BAYOU RECKONING

THE CRANE DIARIES 7

BY APRYL BAKER

BAYOU RECKONING

Limitless Publishing, LLC
Kailua, HI 96734
www.limitlesspublishing.com

Formatting: Book Pages By Design
Cover Design: Deranged Doctor Design

ISBN-13: 978-1-64034-892-9

DEDICATION

For all the fans of Mattie Hathaway
and Eli Malone

1

Saidie Walker

New Orleans, LA

Death is final.

Unless you're me.

Saidie Walker, Necromancer at large. I can bring the dead back, shape them from the very ground itself. And when they arise from the cold comfort of their graves, I restore the echoes of their memories as well.

That's what brought me here to New Orleans, that and a psychopathic vampire who's kidnapping and torturing women. Now Kristoff's gone and taken Emma

Crane. All of that is on me. I should have dealt with Kristoff long before now, but between his craziness and the bad memories here, I stayed away. Now the blood of all those dead women is stained into my soul forever.

There's a soft breeze today, and I take full advantage of it as I stand at the balcony railing outside my room overlooking the gardens. Ezekiel Crane has beautiful gardens. Not nearly as beautiful as Madame's, though. I first met Kristoff in the gardens of Madame's plantation home nestled in the middle of the bayou. I knew he was off then, but I didn't realize just how insane he actually was until later.

Strong arms enfold me, and I lean back into him, relishing how safe Aleric makes me feel.

"Wha's wrong, *Draga*?" His lips trail kisses along the outline of my ear, forcing a shiver through me.

"It's a hell of a mess." I turn and wrap my arms around him, resting my head on his chest. "I should have dealt with this a long time ago."

"*Non, jeune fille*. Dis is no' your fault." His arms tighten. "Doan be doin' dat to yourself. Kristoff is…he's insane. You cain't take his sins on as your own."

But I do. No point in telling Aleric that, though. He won't understand and just argue the point.

I tilt my face up, the rays of the sun bathing it. "It's so warm here."

"*Oui*." He's staring off at nothing, his green eyes lost in memories. "I have missed dis place. I didn't t'ink I would."

"It was your home for a long time. You might have been here against your will, but it became your home. I was born and raised in Georgia. As much as I love West Virginia, I still miss Georgia. It's natural to miss your home."

He nods. "I have even missed my bro'ders. Dey were my family when I had no one else. Madame, she forced us to do awful t'ings, but Lucien, he tried to keep me safe."

"He was your sire?"

"*Oui*. It is a bond dat cain't be broken. I feel him even when he's not here."

"If he were to call you, would you

have to go?"

"I would, *bon fille*. I could no more deny dat pull den I can de pull you have over me."

I wrinkle my nose in disgust. "I don't have any pull over you. I'm the human servant, remember? If anything, you can make me do what you want."

"I would never."

"I know."

We stand there in silence for a few minutes, just enjoying the sun. Aleric has a talisman that allows him to walk in the daylight, thanks to Alex's mom, Alesha. The woman is probably the most powerful witch I know. Alex is technically more powerful than her mother, but she doesn't know all the spells Alesha does, nor does she have the same experience under her belt.

Alesha's magic is controlled, and Alex's is wild and uncontainable at times. I've seen what she can do without even thinking about it, so I understand why the magical community is scared of her. Once she learns a bit more, she's going to be something to see.

4

Mary comes out of the house from below and wanders into the gardens, looking lost and worried. She's somber.

But then that's the current mood of the house. Everyone is on edge, and it feels more like there's been a death in the family than a kidnapping. But I suppose, with Kristoff being the culprit, it might very well turn out to be a funeral rather than a homecoming.

"If it were my little brother he had, I don't know what I'd do."

Aleric brushes a kiss across my forehead. "Doan t'ink of it, *Draga*."

"Even if we do find her before he kills her, will she come back the same?"

Aleric's lips thin. "I doan know."

But he does know. He spent most of his life with Kristoff. He knows better than anyone what the vampire is capable of. He still refuses to talk about what he suffered in that hellish place, but he has nightmares sometimes. Not that he sleeps a lot. Vampires don't technically need sleep, but since Aleric's heart now beats, his body needs to rest every so often.

I'm going to bet Emma will not be the

same person when she comes back. I remember the zombie Kristoff was torturing while I was at Madame's. The Necromancer had put the zombie's soul inside her body so she felt every second of the pain and horror Kristoff put her through. The look in her eyes still haunts me. I wish I could have done something to save her too, but there was no time. Aleric and I fled for our lives and barely escaped.

"De best way to get to her is to get past de crawlers," Aleric says, pulling me from my thoughts.

Crawlers are zombies Madame mutated with her own twisted, dark magic. She wasn't just a Necromancer, but a witch as well. They ooze a black sticky substance that causes intense pain when it touches your skin. It's the kind of pain that imprints into your flesh for the rest of your life. I wouldn't wish it on my worst enemy, including Madame. That's how painful it was.

"They're spelled, and until that's removed, we're stuck. I tried to wake them, and they stayed right where they were. If we can't figure out how to get them out of the water so Alesha can find a work-around of the spell, then I'm not sure how to get to Emma."

"Like you said, *Draga*, it's a hell of a mess."

God's truth, that.

"Saidie?"

"Out here," I call to Alex.

My best friend and I are as different as daylight is to darkness. Alexandria Reed is one of those girls who has no idea how beautiful she is with all that dark hair and eyes so deep a blue they sometimes look black. She's the sweetest person I've ever met. Shy to a fault and self-conscious because she still thinks she might be crazy.

Her grandfather played a head trip on her, putting her into a coma and making her think she was back at the mental institute she pretty much grew up in, thanks to a spell her mother cast on her that backfired. She never knew what was real and what wasn't, and because of that old bastard, she's still in the same position. At least she has us now. We won't let her get lost again.

"Bree just left. One of Mr. Crane's drivers took her to the airport."

Damn, I'd hoped she'd of changed her mind. Sabrina Winters, or Bree to us, is the daughter of one of the three main Families of Power within the witch community. Next to Alesha, she's the most knowledgeable witch we had. She was supposed to help with de-spelling the crawlers.

"How's Jason holding up?"

"My brother is hurt, but I think he's more angry than anything else. He expected Bree to do the right thing and help people who needed it."

"Maybe it's for the best."

"How do you mean?" Alex leans against the railing, her back to the gardens.

"They were getting serious, and we all know she's not his mate. If he'd found his mate and he and Bree were still together, she would have gotten her heart broken."

"I guess." Alex looks up at the cloudless blue sky. "I just hate to see him in so much pain. He really loves her."

"De heart is a strange t'ing." Aleric rests his chin on the top of my head. "It will always find wha' it's lookin' for, even in de middle of de worst pain it's ever felt."

Alex smiles softly. "Like you found Saidie in the hell you were in?"

"*Oui, chèr*, like I found *ma petite sorcière de la mort*, my little death witch."

Alex frowns. "I'm not sure if that's an endearment or not."

"It is." I laugh. "He just has a weird sense of humor."

"Where's Luka?" Aleric asks.

"He went for a run."

That's Alex's way of saying the beast Luka was cursed with needed to get out and hunt. He's never let any of us see it when he transforms, not even Alex, but I'm betting that's a good thing. Luka's scary enough in human form. I'd hate to see him in full monster mode.

"Everybody else?"

"Conner's stuffing his face in the kitchen, and Alesha and Sabien are on the phone with their contacts looking for a solution to the water zombies. Jason's in his room. I checked on him, but he said he wanted to be alone."

"Is dere any news on de girl?" Aleric shifts, and my body automatically shifts with his. It's like we're in tune with each other, two halves of the same whole.

"No. Her boyfriend is pretty much out of it too. They have some kind of weird bond where he feels everything she does, and when she's hurt, he gets the same injury. Maybe not physically, but he still feels it, and that's just as bad, according to Uncle Sabien. Metaphysical wounds can be more dangerous than physical ones."

"And I thought our group was weird. We got nothing on these guys."

"Demons." Alex shakes her head. "I never thought I'd be dealing with demons. I think you're right. These people are weirder than us."

"Did you see that sword her boyfriend pulled?" I still can't get it out of my head. It shined brighter than any light I've ever seen.

"It is one of four holy swords," Aleric tells us. "Wit' all de talk about judging, I t'ink it's de Sword of Trut'. Only a warrior anointed by an Arch Angel can wield dem. Madame spent her life tryin' to find one of de warriors so she cou' steal a sword."

"Why was everyone so worried about the sword, though?"

"De Sword of Trut', it judges dose it touches. If you are found wit'out guilt, you are safe. If dere be som'tin you regret or feel guilty for, den you are judged and cleansed."

"Cleansed?" That doesn't sound so bad.

"You die by de sword so it can cleanse your soul of guilt and regret."

"That's harsh."

I agree with Alex. Harsh doesn't seem the right word, though. It's downright unfair. I feel remorse over stepping on a bug. Would it find me unworthy for killing the bug even though it bit me?

"The Swords are harsh," Aleric says. "Dey have to be, as tools of de holy fait'."

This is why I never really got much into religion. It's all so...so...I don't even have a word for it, but I know it's not something I want to deal with. I'd rather just be me and not worry about anything else.

Time to change the subject.

"So, what do you think Conner meant when he said if we leave, then Emma dies?" Sometimes his visions are cryptic, while at other times they are specific. Last night's was in between those descriptors.

"Emma has to be in the house guarded by all the dead. If we leave, then they won't be able to breach the island before it's too late," Alex says thoughtfully. "I mean, even if Mr. Crane could find a way to break the spell causing them to obey only Kristoff, those things are still dangerous."

"Dey are deadly."

"And if they can't get to the house, then Emma dies." It has to be what Conner meant. It's the only thing that makes sense, really.

"Which is why I think Bree leaving

was selfish." Alex gets this fierce look in her eyes, making the blue glow with that odd color no one can really define. "She's the second most knowledgeable witch among us and could have helped Alesha more than me or Jason, whose magic only just woke up. Leaving means not caring if Emma lives or dies."

"You have to remember that's not how she was raised, Alex. Bree grew up in one of the magical families, taught only to care about the people who matter to them. A stranger means nothing to her."

"I was a stranger to her."

"Not really," I disagree. "The Blackburnes were friends with the Winters family. Bree's grandfather and your mom are really good friends so, to her, you were someone important because your family and hers are allies."

Alex shakes her head stubbornly. "It's still not right."

"Maybe not, but it's the situation we have now, so we have to deal with it."

Her shoulders slump. Like I said, she's the sweetest, kindest person I know, and Bree walking away hurt her. She counts on Bree to be there like she does me, and this is her first taste of what being part of one of the main magical families really means. I get that she doesn't like it one damn bit, but I think it's good for her. She needs to see that people, even her friends, can disappoint her. Hopefully, she'll forgive Bree.

"All right, let's go roust Conner out of the kitchen and find your mom. Maybe they've found something."

As we go back inside and leave the room, I cross my fingers, hoping Alesha and Sabien found a way to remove the spell from the crawlers, because if not, things are going to get a little more dangerous.

Emma Rose

Fulsome Sanitarium, MO

"Once upon a time, there was a beautiful princess named Mathilda who lived in a castle made of chocolate chip cookies upon a hill of fudge. Marshmallow clouds graced stunning blue skies and the rivers ran with blue Kool-Aid."

My mama's blue eyes are bright and glassy, but she smiles at me in the mirror as she brushes my hair.

"She ate cake and ice cream for breakfast, lunch, and dinner, right,

15

Mama?"

"Yes, baby girl. She even had cherries and sprinkles sometimes too."

I giggle and rest my head in my palms. My mama tells the best stories.

The brush glides through my hair. She always does one hundred brush strokes. It makes it all shiny like Mama's. She doesn't do it a lot, so I always love it when she does.

"One day, the princess was in her room drawing pictures of unicorns and puppies when she heard a strange sound. Curious, she left her room and followed the noise outside, careful to not fall off the drawbridge and into the moat of strawberry pudding."

Another giggle escapes. Strawberry pudding. Yuck!

"She went into the gumdrop forest where the trees were made of candy cane bark and giant green sprinkles for the leaves. Deeper and deeper into the forest she walked, until she became tired and stopped to drink from the Kool-Aid river. It was then she saw it."

"What, Mama? What did she see?"

"A giant kitty cat limping along. It was as big as a tiger, but it was only a baby kitty cat."

"Aww...poor kitty. Was it hurt?"

"Yes. It had fallen and hurt its paw. It was scared because it couldn't find its mommy, but Princess Mathilda wasn't scared. She jumped in the river and waded to the other side, telling the big kitty not to be scared. That everything would be okay."

"Did that make the kitty happy?"

"Yes, the kitty was so happy to find a friend that it started to purr so loud it knocked the little princess off her feet. The kitty leaned down and started to lick the princess's face, its whiskers tickling her, and she laughed and laughed."

Mama's fingers dig into my side, and I squeal, laughing as hard as the princess in the story.

Once we stopped laughing, Mama went back to brushing my hair. "Princess Mathilda knew she needed help, so she and the kitty went back to the castle where her mother, Queen Claire, ordered her knights to go out into the forest and

17

find the kitty's mommy. It took them three days, but they brought the kitty's mommy back, along with his brothers and sisters. Queen Claire, having grown to love the kitty as much as her daughter, declared it and its family could live in the castle and roam the gumdrop forest freely. Do you know what happens then?"

"Then they lived happily ever after."

"My beautiful, beautiful baby girl." Mama kisses my cheek and smooths a hand down my hair. "What did Mama tell you?"

I'm not sure what she means, and I look at her in the mirror. Her eyes have gone dark, and she's not smiling anymore.

"There's no such thing as happily ever after." Her fingers wrap around my hair and pull it back tightly like she's going to do the pigtails I like, but she doesn't. She keeps pulling my hair tighter and tighter until it hurts.

"Mama, stop, it hurts!" I try to wriggle free, but she makes this noise that scares me, and this time when I look at her in the mirror, she's smiling again, but it's

not my mama's smile. It's a scary smile full of long teeth.

Mama leans down, her nose running along my cheek.

She smells bad.

Her eyes are glowing red in the mirror.

"Bad girls who don't follow the rules don't end up with happily ever afters." She pulls my hair tighter, forcing my head back, and I cry out, trying to get away.

What's wrong with her?

"Do you know what happens to bad little girls?"

"No," I whisper.

"They get punished."

A knife appears in her hand, and my eyes widen. I'm afraid of that knife, but I don't know why. What's she going to do with it?

"Mama, please, I'm scared."

"Good, you need to be scared, Mattie Louise. You need to be very, very afraid of me."

The knife blade comes down, sinking into the soft flesh of my shoulder, twisting. Screaming, I kick out, but Mama laughs. She pulls the blade out and stabs me again and again and again.

"This is what happens when you don't follow the rules."

I jerk awake, my breath coming in short gasps as nothing but darkness greets me. I'm shaking, and not from the cold either, even though it's got to be well below freezing. No, it's the images that followed me out of the dream. I remember that day. It's one of the few good memories I have of my mama. She was high as a kite but still lucid enough to understand I was in the apartment. I loved that day. We played and played and played, and then she sat me down after a bath to brush my hair. I'd forgotten the story, though.

Kristoff took a good memory and turned it into a nightmare.

With no more dead man's blood, I have no way of keeping him out of my memories or my dreams. With all the things I've gone through, I'm dreading what's coming. He knows everything. He's been in my head, sifted through my memories, and fed upon my pain as he drank it all down with my blood.

My blood. It leads me to another fear. What will drinking my blood do for him? Will he absorb some of my gifts? I don't know. It's something I should have asked after the first time, but none of us thought to question the ramifications of that. Not even Zeke.

Turning over, I curl up under the blanket and try to get a little warm. Zeke must be going crazy. He's got to be remembering how it felt when he came home all those years ago to discover me gone from my nursery, taken by the woman he'd hired to care for me. He's only spoken about it to me once, and the look in his eyes had caused my heart to ache for the pain he'd gone through.

And Dan. God, he must be out of his mind. I reach out again, attempting to feel him, but there's nothing there except emptiness. The cold void of the unknown. My only saving grace is that he doesn't know what I'm going through, what I'm feeling. I'm betting whatever this collar is, it's cut him off from me too. He'd drive himself insane if he felt even a fraction of my fear and not be able to do anything about it.

He's safe, I reassure myself. Silas won't let anything happen to him because he knows if it does, then I die too.

Maybe.

Rhea shared her own protections with me, and now Silas thinks if Dan dies, those protections might save my life. I'm not sure I'd survive if that happened, though.

There's a soft scuffle, and I sit up, looking around even though it's pointless. It's so dark in here I can't even see an inch in front of my face. My biggest fear is rats, and every little noise I hear, I'm afraid it's rats. The place is so old there has to be a small army of the rodents on the premises. My nerves are on edge, and my breathing is rapid. I've grown to hate the dark over the last few days.

"Easy, Hilda."

My head swivels, but all I see is darkness. Shaking my head, I lie back down, dismissing the voice as a hallucination of sorts. I'd dreamed of Eli Malone the last time I drifted off to sleep. He was my personal Guardian Angel and Dan's little brother. He died to protect me back in Charlotte. There's no way Eli's here. Just me wishing it were so.

That doesn't make it so, though.

It would be nice to have my furnace back. Eli told me that he'd be whatever I needed him to be. What I usually needed was to feel warm, and his body would become my own personal furnace. As cold as I am now, I'd welcome it.

I miss him. More than I admit to anyone, including Dan. I loved Eli with my whole heart in a way that was unique and special for only him. His death still cripples me with grief and guilt. I don't talk about that either. If it wasn't for me, he'd never have been cursed. Well, technically, it wasn't me specifically. Silas had started cultivating his bloodline to defeat the Fallen Angel Deleriel, and Deleriel, being Deleriel, put his own safeguards in place. Eli's family curse was just one of those safeguards.

I wonder a lot if Deleriel saw into the

future and knew I was coming. It would explain why he cursed Eli's family bloodline to kill the person they loved the most. That was me for Eli. Instead of killing me, he killed himself to keep from harming me. I'll never get his blood off my hands, and I don't want it off. I should have been able to find a way around that curse. I should have saved him. He was a good person. Honest and kind. Me? Not so much. I'm a better person than I was, but I will still do what I have to in order to protect my family. I'd kill to keep them safe.

Eli should have lived, and I should have died.

Even admitting that hurts because it means Dan would have died, but maybe we both shouldn't be here. All the powers that be say we're abominations and that our choosing each other caused all sorts of horrible things. We were both selfish.

One day, that knowledge will hit Dan, and when it does, he's not going to take it well. One day, he'll be faced with the consequences of what we did. Meg died because of us, but I have a feeling there are worse things out there than the death of my best friend and Dan's old girlfriend. Bad things that will come for us and make us face our choices.

God, I'm being morose. It has to be because I'm trapped here and at the mercy of a deranged vampire. He's been in my thoughts, and he's probably manipulating me, forcing me to think about the things I do my best to forget. Things I feel guilty about.

Even though I know we should have died, I will never regret saving Dan. He's the entire reason I'm alive now, the reason I'm becoming the kind of person he deserves. He's the reason my heart beats and the reason I understand love. He's everything to me.

So, despite my own guilt, despite my knowing we should be dead, I'll fight to my last breath to save him. And that means staying alive until I can get out of here. Or Dan finds me. I'm not going to bet on that, though. I grew up on my own, and I know how to survive. I'll survive one way or another.

"There's the fighter I know."

My head snaps up, peeking out from under the covers. That was Eli's voice. I know it as well as I know my own. But I don't see him.

Maybe all this darkness and being utterly alone is getting to me. Silence is just as much of an assault on the mind as blaringly loud music for days on end. I think that's why prisons have solitary confinement. I'm fairly sure the prisons would say otherwise, but it's my opinion, and I'll keep it.

I'm so tired, but sleep taunts me. It teases me into a lulled state, and then some noise will interrupt me, like the sound of rats or the odd noise outside the door to this room. I know what's out there. I saw them. They know who I am. All ghosts do. They're drawn to me like a sailor to a lighthouse. If it weren't for the iron encasing me, they'd be in here.

I've never been without my power to see a ghost since I woke up with the ability at five years old. At first, I'd been so scared I didn't know what to do, and then I figured out if I ignored them, they'd go away. Still, I'd always known where they were because I could see them. I never realized how important that was to me until now. Not being able to see them is scarier than seeing the mangled and disfigured echoes of who they were and how they died.

And with a basement full of ghosts that had been insane and murderous in life, not having my abilities makes this a thousand times more terrifying. I used to hate my ability, but I've grown to understand it's as much a gift as a curse. I'm able to help lost souls move on, to cross over and rejoin their loved ones on the other side. At least I hope so. I've got no idea what's actually on the other side. I might be a living reaper, but that doesn't mean I've actually taken a soul to the other side. Kane always did that.

A stab of pain slices through my heart. Kane's somewhere being punished, and I don't think that means detention. Reapers can be cruel because most of them don't care about anything except their purpose. Kane cared. He helped me more times than I can count, and I have to find a way to rescue him.

One more reason to survive this place and Kristoff.

I can't save Kane if I don't get out of here.

I wish I wore a watch. At least I'd know what time it is and when I can expect the next torture session to begin. From here on, I'm always going to wear one.

Strange to be thinking of my lack of a watch when I have so many other things to worry about, but the mind is strange itself. Or the brain, I guess. I read once that humans only use about twenty percent of their brain. Maybe I use twenty-one percent or something like that with my reaping abilities. Still, the brain is a mystery, especially for those of us with special abilities.

"Hilda, you need to stop thinking about nonsense. We have to talk."

No, no, no. Eli is not here. He's dead. He crossed over. I watched him cross over. He can't be here.

"I *am* here, Mattie. I promise. Open your eyes and really look."

This is another of Kristoff's tricks. I'm

asleep, and he's messing with me. To use Eli against me, that is plain cruel. He knows how much Eli meant to me and the awful, crippling guilt I carry with me because of his death.

Warmth wraps around me, so bright and hot, it chases the cold away. I haven't felt this warm since Eli was alive. A tear leaks out as that heartbreaking grief invades my soul. I miss him so much.

"I'm right here. Just open your eyes and look." The whispered words compel me to do as he asks.

Pulling the lone blanket down, I open my eyes and focus on the warmth surrounding me. It's a heat I remember well. Only Eli could warm me through, chase away the cold that seeped into my bones from all the ghost energy I carry around with me. Only Eli burned me up in an instant blaze when his lips touched mine.

As my eyes adjust to the darkness, a shape takes form in front of me. At first, it's just a shadow in the darkness, but as I stare and remember everything about Eli and the way he made me feel, the outline fills in, and soon, those beautiful aqua eyes are shining at me from a face that hints at mischief and devilry. Blond hair streaked with tones of caramel and toffee falls over his left eye, and he brushes it aside.

It really is him.

But how?

He shakes his head and smiles. "Really, Hilda? We just had this conversation last night. What did I promise you?"

"You'd always find me."

"That's right. Just because I died doesn't mean I stopped being your Guardian Angel. That's a bond not even death can break. When you truly need me, I'll always find you."

"Can you go find Dan or Zeke and tell them where I am?"

"No. You're the only person who can see me. I did die, Hilda."

"My dad and Mary...they can see..."

He's shaking his head before I even get the words out, and the hope that sprang to life dies an agonizing death.

"I'm *your* Guardian Angel, not theirs.

That's the only reason you can still see me with that thing around your neck."

"Are you a figment of my imagination or something? My freaked-out mind conjure you up to keep me from being so scared?"

He grins. "Does it matter?"

No, I guess not. "Did you see the crazy ghosts?"

That wipes the grin off his face. "Those are some seriously dangerous ghosts. It's a good thing you're encased in iron."

Which makes me think Eli is a figment of my imagination. He's dead, so he's technically a ghost. Ghosts can't cross an iron barrier.

"You're forgetting I have Angel blood. I'm not an ordinary ghost."

"Are you reading my mind?"

He laughs, and the sound is a balm to my shredded nerves. God, I missed him so much.

"I'm a ghost, so yes, I am hearing your thoughts the same way any other ghost can communicate with you."

"If you're a ghost, why are you still a

furnace?" My fingers aren't numb anymore. The heat he's giving off is heavenly.

"Because I'm what you need me to be, and you need a heat source right now." He comes closer and drops down on the mattress, taking my hand in his. "Why haven't you healed your broken bones yet?"

"Because I can't." No use in pointing out he shouldn't be able to hold my hand as he's a ghost, but he's as solid as I am. Maybe the Angel blood?

"Yes, you can."

"No, Eli. I really can't. There's a locked door in my head that's blocking my healing abilities. It's locked so tight not even my mother can unlock it."

"Your mother? I thought she wanted you dead?"

"No, not Georgina. Rhea."

"You lost me, Hilda."

I explain to him that Rhea is my metaphysical mother and how she shared her protections with me since mine are out of commission. I'd probably be dead right now if she hadn't. Kristoff took a lot of blood when he fed from me. I was woozy most of the day. I still am, really.

"Girl, I have missed your drama."

"I don't do drama on purpose."

"I know, but it sure does make things more interesting around you." His eyes sparkle with amusement, and that old pain hits me right in the chest. Grief has an awful way of surprising you at the worst moment.

"Hey, now, what's wrong?"

"I just really, really missed you."

Eli pulls me into a hug, and I swear I can smell his soap. He always smelled like lemons. His mother buys the brand from one of those all-natural online stores. It doesn't comfort me, though. It just makes the tears well up, and a sob breaks free. God, did I miss him. I never let myself think about just how much I miss him because of Dan, but I really, really do.

He holds me for the longest time before finally pulling back, his expression turning fierce. "No more crying."

"I didn't used to cry at all." A hiccup

escapes.

"I know, Hilda, and that's the girl I need right now."

"What do you mean?"

"You've gone soft."

"I have not!" Well, maybe a little. I'll admit that to myself, but not to anyone else.

"Yes, you have. Don't get me wrong, that's not a bad thing in normal circumstances, but you're dealing with someone who will take every vulnerability and kindness you have and use it against you. You need to go back to being the old Mattie, the girl who would sooner hurt you than look at you."

"I didn't like that person very much, Eli. I don't want to go back to being her."

"You won't survive this if you don't." The grimness of his tone sends a shiver down my spine. "You've gotten so used to taking care of everyone else, putting them first, you've forgotten how to take care of yourself. Or you don't care."

"That's not true. I always worry about me because of Dan."

"Hilda, I'm not talking physically. I'm

thinking about your mental state. Kristoff will use everything you've been through, the relationships you've built against you. He'll turn them against you in your head. You can't let him do that. The old you was as much about keeping your emotions locked down as you were about physical violence. That's what I'm talking about. You have to go cold again. You have to shove it all down and react to nothing. You have to be the foster kid again in order to be the person you are now when you get out of here."

I know he's right. He's only saying what I've been thinking since that first night. Kristoff already took one of the best memories I have of my mother and turned it into a nightmare. Who knows what else he can do to me?

But how to go backward? How to lock everything away?

"I'm not sure how to do that anymore."

"Yes, you are. You just don't want to. That place scares you because when you go there, you could kill someone without a blink of an eye or an ounce of regret. You're afraid to be that person, to be who you were born to be."

"I wasn't born to be a killer, Eli."

"But that's who you are, Hilda. You have a darkness in you, and as much as you want to run from it, as much as you want to hide, you can't. You've only ever embraced it when it comes to keeping my brother alive. The person you have to save this time is yourself. It's not a question or a choice. It's a must."

I don't want to. It was so hard to get to where I am now. He doesn't know what he's asking of me.

"Eli…"

He takes my face in his hands and looks me in the eye. "What is my job as your Guardian Angel?"

"To be whatever I need you to be."

He leans his forehead against mine. "You know what you have to do, and my job is to make you listen, even if it's not what you want to hear."

"It's not that easy."

"No, Hilda, it's not. But I'm here now, and I'm not leaving."

"Promise?"

"Promise." He kisses the tip of my

nose. "No matter what, I'm not leaving."

"You left me before."

He smiles. "I was stupid, but I'm not anymore. I'm here, and I'll be here until you don't need me."

I believe him.

Eric

New Orleans

"Here you are."

I look up to see Ethan strolling in. I never even heard the door open. I'd closed it because I wanted to be left alone, even by him. *Especially* by him.

"Man, you missed it. That Sabien dude, he put Dan to sleep with just a word. Coolest thing ever."

Ethan thinks all things magic and paranormal are cool. He hasn't seen the things I have, though. If he had, maybe he wouldn't be so starry-eyed all the time when we talk about the supernatural. I wish I didn't know the things I do. It'd be easier to sleep at night.

He falls down on the couch beside me. "What are we watching?"

I have no clue. I'd just turned the TV on for background noise. The volume is so low, it's just barely audible. I'm not in the mood for much of anything.

"No idea," I mutter.

He picks the remote up and starts channel surfing. It irritates me. "I was watching that."

"Dude, you just said you had no idea what was on." He settles on one of those home improvement shows Mattie loves so much. I'd purposefully kept it off that channel. I don't want anything that reminds me of her.

I snatch the remote out of his hands and turn the TV off.

"What is your problem?"

"I don't have one," I snap.

"Why are you in the basement, anyway?" Ethan's brown eyes are full of concern, and that just bothers me more.

"Because I wanted to be left alone, and

I thought no one would bother me down here." I stare pointedly at him.

He frowns. "What's wrong?"

"What are you, my mother or something?" I slouch back on the couch and cross my arms, my expression daring him to keep talking.

Ethan, being Ethan, ignores my warming. "If I have to be, yeah. You've been in this mood since we found out Mattie took off. She did that on her own. It's not your fault."

Like I don't know that? It's not the point anyway.

"Ethan, go back upstairs. I'm not in the mood for this."

"Tough. You and I are going to have this out."

"What the hell are you talking about?"

"You owe a dollar to the swear jar."

Pain lances through me. Why did she run off without telling me? Why? She knows I would have gone with her. I would have done everything in my power to protect her.

"Damn, I didn't think…" Ethan trails off and raises a hand, almost like he wants to touch me, but lets it fall. "I'm sorry. It's just habit to say that."

I know. We all say it now. Cass or Robert are usually the only ones owing money to the swear jar these days. Mattie hates cussing. She doesn't do it and prefers no one around her do it either. Jesus help you if you take the Lord's name in vain around that girl. She usually doesn't say much about other people cussing that aren't us, but if she hears "GD," she lets whoever said it know exactly how she feels about that particular swear word. She's fearless around strangers.

I miss her.

What's she going through? What is that bastard doing to her? I want to get my hands on him so I can choke him to death slowly. I want…

Ethan snaps his fingers in front of my face. "Eric, you're starting to worry me."

"I'm not your problem."

"You're my best friend, so yeah, that makes you my problem."

I turn away from him, staring at the bookshelves on the wall opposite us. This is Zeke's personal getaway. I found it a few months ago, and he said I could use it whenever I wanted to get away too. He and I talked about the feelings I'm dealing with. He didn't judge; he just listened and told me I could talk to him about it whenever I needed to.

I was embarrassed later. Zeke can make a person tell him the truth. It's one of his gifts. You can't lie to him. He saw I was struggling and forced me to talk. Not that I hold it against him. I needed to talk. It helped.

"I'm not a woman who sits and talks about feelings. I said I want to be alone, and I'd think being my *best friend,* you'd respect that."

He's quiet for a full minute. I resist the urge to turn and look. Ethan's important to me, and as much as I hate pushing him away, I need to be alone. Him being here only makes how I'm feeling worse.

"It's because I'm your best friend I'm not respecting that BS you're spewing. I know you're hurting for something you're not responsible for. Em…Mattie wouldn't want you sitting down here going through this alone."

My fist clenches. I want to hurt something so bad right now.

"Tell me what you need. Alcohol? I'll get it. Want to pound something? Hit me. I may not be the football player you are, but I got some weight on me. I can take it. Just tell me what you need, and I'll do it."

"You want me to hit you?" I ask, incredulous. He's not wrong about our size difference. I have a football player's physique, which means I'm taller than he is, and I have a good fifty pounds on him too. I move people twice his size out of my way on the field. Ethan wouldn't stand a chance against me. I'd knock him flat out with one punch.

"If that's what you need, yeah. I may end up with bruises and a black eye, but I'm game if it'll get you out of this mood."

He's crazy.

"I'm not hitting you, man." Letting out a sigh, I turn back around, hoping he's not serious, but I can tell from his expression he is.

"I can take it."

"Yeah, I know, but I'm still not hitting you."

"Then do you want beer or liquor? We can get wasted and forget for a little while."

If I get wasted, I might say things we'll both regret later. It's why I don't drink so much anymore. Even living in a frat house, I'm usually the designated sober person who answers the door and makes sure people get home safe and that stupid shit doesn't go on at the house like drunk girls ending up in rooms they wouldn't be in if they were sober.

"No, I don't want anything."

"Except for Mattie."

Why does his voice sound strange?

"You don't understand."

"No, I don't." It's his turn to cross his arms. "What's up with you and her anyway? Are you in love with her or something? Because if you are, don't let Dan see it. He'll rip you in half."

"I do love her."

His eyes narrow to slits. "He's going to tear you limb from limb."

Closing my eyes, I let my head fall back onto the couch cushion. "I'm not *in love* with her, but I think once upon a time I was."

"She said the two of you kissed once." His voice has gone all gravelly. I love the sound of it when it does that, so I keep my eyes closed. He'll see what I don't want him to.

"She and Jake dated in high school." I clear my throat. "I don't remember any of that, though."

"The car accident," Ethan murmurs.

"Car accident?" I sit up and open my eyes. "What are you talking about?"

"Your dad told me you'd been in an accident, and you had amnesia as a result. I assumed it was a car accident."

I bark out a laugh. If I were them, I'd think of it as an accident too, but it wasn't.

"I wasn't in a car accident."

"Then what happened?"

"Jake's brother shot him."

"Say what?" His mouth drops open. "Your brother shot you?"

He doesn't know I'm not Jake, that

I've never been Jake.

"I don't want to talk about it."

"Sure, okay." He nods and settles back, throwing an arm over the back of the couch. His fingers graze the nape of my neck, and a full body shiver goes through me. I jerk away like he's slapped me, and he looks hurt.

"Look, Ethan…"

"No." He holds up his hand to cut off whatever I was about to say. "We're hashing this out. Mary needs you to get out of this funk. The only person who's there for her right now is Nathaniel, and I trust him about as far as I can throw him. She won't talk to me, or *I'd* be there for her."

"You like her?" I ask, not able to hold back the surliness of the question. Of course he likes her. Mary's gorgeous with all that blonde hair and blue eyes she's got going on.

"Well, yeah. She's cool."

My shoulders slump. I didn't want him to answer me. Not really. I'm not sure how I'll deal if the two of them hook up. I might even transfer to UNC Chapel

Hill. Or go back home to Charlotte. Dealing with Jake's parents would be easier than dealing with Ethan and Mary getting together.

"Seriously, can you just go away? I'm not in the mood for company right now."

"Why are you so pissed off all of a sudden?"

"Because I'm worried, okay? She's out there suffering God knows what, and there's not a damn thing I can do about it!" I roar, letting out some of my frustration and pain all at once. "I've been watching out for her since she was a kid. That's what I do. I take care of her. And I'm here, helpless, while she's getting hurt."

"That, right there, what are you talking about? What do you mean, taking care of her since she was a kid? She was in foster care in New Jersey, and you lived in North Carolina. I thought the two of you met in high school." His face is red, his own anger surfacing. "You're both always saying cryptic shit like that, and all she'll say about it is to ask you, and when I do, you won't talk about it either.

I'm done getting the brush off."

I bend over, my head between my knees as my breath comes out in short gasps. What did I do? I just shouted the very thing I've been hiding from him. He's not going to let this go.

"Shit."

"Exactly so." Ethan bends down. "Dude, you okay?"

I shake my head. "Go get us some beers. This is going to take a while."

He starts to go upstairs, and I stop him, pointing to Zeke's mini fridge. He keeps it stocked with Sam Adams. I never thought I'd drink anything but Budweiser, but that stuff has grown on me.

Ethan hands me a beer and sits back down, waiting.

"You're sure you want to know this? Once I tell you, there's no unknowing it."

"Yeah, I'm sure. I hate being the odd man out when it comes to the information you, Mary, and Mattie share. I feel like you guys don't trust me enough to let me in on the big secret. It gets old fast."

"Sometimes not knowing is easier than

knowing. Sometimes it's the only way to protect the people we love."

He sighs. "I'd rather know the truth than go crazy wondering all the time. I can take it."

I hope so. I'd hate to lose him. He's as important to me as Mattie.

"My name is Eric Lawrence Cameron. I was born on July twenty-forth, nineteen ninety-five."

"What?" He rears back. "I'm not in the mood for jokes, Eric. I'm serious. I want to know the truth."

"I promise I'm not messing with you. Just be quiet and listen, okay?"

He nods slowly, but I can tell he's not sure if I'm serious.

Sometimes I wish I could be Jake, that I could have his memories instead of my own. It would make everything easier for all of us, but especially for Jake's parents.

"My mother died in a fire when I was a baby, and my grandmother took me. She raised me until I was fourteen when she died from a stroke. I went into foster care after that. It's where I met Mattie. She was just a little kid who tried to defend herself against everyone and everything, but she didn't know how to fight. I remember thinking what a beautiful little girl she was, and I got scared for her. She was exactly the type of kid certain men preyed on, the kind of sick, twisted men you find more often than not in the system. So, I taught her how to fight."

She really was a beautiful kid, and I worried so much for her, not only because of her looks, but her attitude. She hated being in the system and acted out. She'd shifted through more homes than most of the kids I knew in the system combined. It didn't bode well for her, and I decided to do what I could to help her. I might not have been able to change her attitude, but I could help her learn to defend herself if necessary. And that's what I'd done while she was in the same home as me. When she left, I only hoped she'd use the skills I taught her to protect herself.

"Hey, you okay?"

I blink, coming out of my thoughts. "Sorry, just thinking about the past.

Where was I?"

"How you met Mattie."

I nod and take a long drink of beer. Maybe we should have broken out the actual liquor for this conversation.

"She was moved to another foster home, and I lost track of her. I was adopted about a year later to a couple I came to love. They were the parents of my best friend, Derek James. He convinced them to take me in, and they were good people who took care of me. Derek and I started playing basketball when we moved to Charlotte, and it was after a game that I was taken."

"Taken?"

I remember everything that was done to me in the weeks before my death. It haunts me. I have nightmares about it, and I hate talking about it because it makes the nightmares so much worse. But for Ethan, I'll brave my demons and hope he's still there when I'm done.

"I went out the side door like some of the team did to escape the madhouse. We'd won, and everyone was cheering. It was easier to get to where I'd parked my car, but I made it about five steps when someone hit me from behind, and I blacked out. When I woke up, I was tied down to a chair."

"What?" Ethan whispers, shocked.

"I was blindfolded, and no matter how I struggled, I couldn't get free. I'm not sure how long I was alone before he came in. I was scared, expecting him to say something about keeping quiet. But he never said a word. For the weeks I was there, he never once spoke to me. I got food and water once every couple days, but after about a week, it was hard to keep it down."

Ethan makes a strangled sound, and I flinch away from it. As hard as this is to hear, it's even harder to relive.

"He tortured me, messed up my face so bad it was unrecognizable. Broken bones, stab wounds, you name it, he did it. I lived in pain. I begged him to stop, to tell me why he was doing this to me. I even begged for death, but he never said a word to me."

"I don't…"

I hold up a hand. I need to get this out.

"The day I heard the gun cock, I said a prayer of thanks to God that it was finally ending. But it didn't. He shot me in the head, and I died, but I wasn't gone. I stayed there in that dank basement, and it was only then I saw that the man who killed me wasn't a man, but a woman. She stood over my dead body and smiled."

I take another long drink of my beer and glance at Ethan. He's horrified. I hate that I have to burden him with this, but he's right. He needs to know.

"You stayed here, though? Why?"

"I didn't know at first. One minute I was there staring at the woman, and the next I was in the car with her and then in her home. I was attached to her."

"She took something of yours, and it bound your spirit to it."

"Yes, but I still don't know what that was."

"I'm so sorry, Eric."

Closing my eyes, I take a deep breath. "I wasn't always with her. Sometimes I went to the dark place, the place I died. It was cold, pitch black and terrifying. And soon, another girl appeared in that basement, tied to the same chair. She was about ten, and the woman tortured her. I tried to help her. I tried so hard, but I was a ghost. There was nothing I could do. She tortured and killed more kids, and when their spirits passed to the ghost plane, I took them and did everything I could to keep them safe from the dangers our new world had. There are things there that not even Mattie has seen. Things I don't want her to ever know about."

Ethan remains quiet while I down what's left of my beer. He gets up and brings me back another one. I nod in appreciation.

"I was roaming the halls of the woman's home, checking on the children she had there, when Mattie showed up. I knew who she was the moment I saw her. She'd grown up, but she still looked the same. I was terrified for her."

"So, the woman was a foster parent, then?" Ethan settles back against the couch, scooting a little closer to me. I press myself away from him. He looks hurt, but I need my distance to finish this.

"Yes. Her name was Mrs. Olsen. I don't know her first name. I'm sure Mattie does, but I never went out of my way to learn much about her. I had more than enough memories of my own. She started taking foster kids in after she murdered me. Maybe it was guilt, maybe it was something else. All I know is she never harmed the children in her care. All her victims came from elsewhere."

"It probably was guilt, then." Ethan threw his legs up on the coffee table. "She hurt kids, and so by taking care of those less fortunate, it probably cleared her of her trespass. At least in her own mind."

"Trespass?"

"My grandfather was a pastor. It's a word he used all the time for sin. I know how you feel about the whole God thing, so I used that word instead."

"Does it bother you that I don't believe in God?"

He shook his head. "One thing Grampa always said is the same thing Mattie says. Just because you don't believe in God doesn't mean He doesn't believe in you.

So it's fine with me that you're skeptical. When we go into dangerous situations, I pray for you as well as the rest of us, and I know you'll be protected."

I can't help smiling. "It's weird hearing you talk about this stuff." It's also really nice to know he cares enough to keep me in his prayers. Whether I believe in those prayers or not is moot. He does, and he includes me.

He shrugs. "I dunno. I guess I just don't want to shove it down people's throats, ya know? It's enough for me to know I believe. I don't have to talk about it all the time."

I pat his leg. "You can talk about it around me. I don't mind."

"Thanks, man."

"Back to the story. You sidetracked me."

"Sorry." He shoots me an impish grin.

If he only knew what that grin does to me.

"Mattie was fine for a long time, but it was the night of the party that things got bad. One of her foster sisters, Sally, went missing, and Mattie saw her ghost that night. She was like a dog with a bone. She knew the girl hadn't run away and set about trying to prove it. I did everything I could to scare her away, even showing myself to her. Those of us who can see the ghosts that roam this plane see them as they were when they died. I was scary, my face mutilated. She still didn't back off. I tried screaming at her, but it hurt her, which was not my intent. It's how she ended up in the hospital and met Dan."

"She told me about meeting him. Said she just verbal vomited everything she didn't want him to know. Blamed it on his, and I quote, 'warm puppy-dog eyes.'"

"She's always been a sucker for that." I smile ruefully. That girl has a thing for eyes. "When he agreed to help her, I was so happy. If she disappeared or turned up dead, he'd know it was more than just another foster kid going missing. Mrs. Olsen also knew he was hanging around, and that gave me more relief than anything else. Surely she wouldn't do anything to her while an actual cop was being buddy-buddy with Mattie."

"But I take it she did?"

"Mattie saw Sally again and followed her to where Mary was being held. Mrs. Olsen was there and knocked her out, taking her down to the basement. I will never be able to describe the feelings I had watching Mattie get tortured and not being able to do anything to help her. I have as many nightmares about that as I do about my own experiences."

"You really love her, don't you?"

"I do."

We're both silent for a few minutes as we sip on our beers. Ethan doesn't push. He knows I'll start talking when I'm ready. Another trait I share with Mattie.

"Mattie has the best survival skills of anyone I know. She was able to escape, and she ended up pushing Mrs. Olsen over the upstairs railing, which incapacitated her, but Mattie was really hurt. She was dying. She'd sent me to find Dan, and I did everything I could to show him where she was. He has good instincts and came looking. He found her and gave her CPR. He kept her heart beating until the paramedics got there. He's never told her that. But she came back, and in the end, they saved both her and Mary. I stayed on this plane to keep an eye on her. Girl might be able to survive a lot, but she also got into more trouble than anyone I'd ever met."

"You stayed? Does that mean you could have passed over to the other side?"

I nod. "Yes. Mattie opened the doorway for us before she passed out. I was afraid to leave her, so I stayed."

"That's…I'm not sure what to say, Eric."

"Do you want to know the rest of it?"

"Yes."

"It's not all hearts and flowers, as Mary would say."

"Nothing ever is, but I need to know."

He does, but that doesn't mean the rest of it will be easy. I just hope he understands.

I pull my legs up against my chest as I prepare myself to confess everything to Ethan. It's not something I'd ever planned on doing, but losing Mattie has shown me that I need to man up. Life is short, and living in fear and uncertainty isn't how I want to live anymore. If Ethan leaves, then he leaves. But at least I will have told him the truth.

"When a ghost is on this plane for a long time, we start to go mad. Our feelings turn against us. We become enraged at not being alive, at not being able to be seen by all the people passing by. We hate that the living can do all the things we can't. That anger turns us into vengeful spirits, taking our pain and anger out on the living."

"And you started to turn into one of those?" Ethan asks, turning so he's facing me.

"Yeah. I was free of Mrs. Olsen. I'm not sure how that happened, but I was able to go where I wanted. Without a purpose, I had nothing to center me. I mean, looking out for Mattie was sort of a purpose, but I found myself wandering more and more. I could feel myself changing, and I wasn't sure how to stop it."

"That sounds scary."

"You have no idea. I'd seen vengeful spirits, and I didn't want to be one of those. I remember I got this feeling right in the center of my chest. It burned, and I knew something was wrong with Mattie. I'm not sure how I knew. I just did. She was easy to find. Her light glows like a lighthouse for a ghost. She was in a house with a ghost who was feeding off her energy, and she couldn't stop him. She needed energy, a boost so strong she could break the bonds he'd trapped her in. I knew I was going vengeful, and I didn't want that, so I told her to take me, to reap me."

"What?" Ethan's eyes were wide and horrified. "You wanted her to kill you?"

"I was already dead, Ethan. There was nothing left for me except madness. I could help her, and that's exactly why I chose to stay here."

"You sacrificed yourself to save her."

"It saved us both."

Ethan downs his beer and gets up for another one. I haven't touched the second one he gave me earlier. The first one steadied my nerves enough for this conversation.

"The next thing I remember is waking up in a hospital in a lot of pain. The doctors said I'd been shot. I didn't remember that. I didn't remember anything. Not my name, not my parents, not my life. I was a blank slate. I was so scared. Jake's parents tried their best to reassure me and told me how much they loved me, but they were strangers."

"That sucks, man."

I snort. Sucks isn't the right word.

Terrified doesn't even begin to describe how I felt not being able to even remember my own name. It's a feeling I never want to have again.

"Mattie came by to see me, and it was like the sky opened up and shined a ray of sunlight down upon her. She looked familiar. In a sea of strangers, she looked so familiar to me. And I knew her name. Jake's mom was beside herself thinking his memories were coming back, but they didn't. Because I wasn't Jake. I'll never *be* Jake."

"I don't understand. How did you end up in a body if you were a ghost?"

"Mattie reaped me. My energy stayed inside her. When Jake was shot, he died, and his soul moved on, but the paramedics were able to revive him. He was on life support with no brain function. Mattie took a chance and put my soul in his body, and it worked."

"How did you remember who you were?"

"Something happened when she touched me. There was this bright light, and I saw my life, who I'd been while I was alive and all I'd done while I was dead. She not only gave me back my life, she gave me back my memories. I feel bad for Jake's parents. I think they keep hoping I'll remember them, and I can't. Maybe his memories are locked in my head somewhere, but I have no access to them. It would be easier for all of us if I could remember."

"That's got to be hard on you guys."

"I'm pretty sure Jake's mom knows the truth. That day in the hospital when I got my memory back, she was listening outside, and she told me it didn't matter if I was the old Jake or someone new. She'd love me anyway. Only it's not me she loves. It's this body, the image of her son. And his father is always trying to tell me stories of Jake's life. He misses his son. They both want that person back, and that's just as bad as being in a foster home where you know you're not loved."

"But you are loved." Ethan reaches out and takes my hand. "You have Mattie and Mary. You have Zeke and his parents. And you have me. We're your family, Eric."

I snatch my hand away from him, and he draws back, hurt. I don't mean to hurt him, but it felt so good to hold his hand. I've fantasized about it for months. I tried so damn hard not to have feelings for him because that's not who I was. I didn't like guys. But this body does. I hate being trapped in it sometimes.

"Do you not want to be my family?" Ethan asks.

"It's not that."

"Then what is it? I'm getting sick and damn tired of you acting like I have the plague or something."

Taking a deep breath, I turn and look at him. "There's more to the story you should know."

"Does it explain what you just did there?"

"Yeah."

"Then tell me."

Easier said than done.

"It's hard, man. I'm not sure how you'll take it."

"Then just spit it out. The more you chew on it, the worse you're gonna feel."

He's not wrong.

"When Jake went out with Mattie, he never pressured her for sex. He never even asked for it."

"And?" he prompted when I didn't go on.

"There was a reason for that."

"Okay?"

Why does this have to be so damn hard?

"Jake didn't like girls. He liked guys."

Ethan's eyes go round, and I can see the wheels turning in his head, but I can't really read his expression.

"I never even thought about a guy like that. I was as straight as they came. But…"

"But being in Jake's body meant you had to deal with his feelings."

I nod. "Yeah. It's been rough. Zeke's been talking to me about it, and it's helped, but I still have freak-out moments."

"So, you don't find women attractive anymore?"

"No, I do. I'm still me, but…"

"I get it." Ethan nods as if he knows exactly what I mean.

"Do you, though, Ethan? Do you understand what it's like to wake up one day and find a man attractive when your whole life you only liked women?"

He frowns.

"Do you know what it's like to have feelings for a guy, feelings that tear you up inside because part of you thinks they're wrong?"

"You have feelings for a guy?" Ethan's frown deepens, and his eyes take on an edge. "Who?"

"It doesn't matter," I mutter. "What matters is this is something you can't understand."

"Don't treat me like a moron," he snaps, finally getting angry. "I can understand just fine. You're dealing with things you never expected to deal with. Things you don't want to deal with. You're frustrated, angry, scared. I'm around you all the time, Eric. I see the things you're going through. Only an idiot wouldn't understand."

Setting my beer on the table, I lean forward and drop my head into my hands. "Look, I've told you all of it. Every last detail. Will you…"

"No, you haven't told me all of it. Who's this guy you have feelings for? Do I know him?"

"What does it matter?"

"It matters." Ethan takes a deep breath. "Trust me, Eric, it matters."

I shake my head. I'd planned to confess my feelings, but I'm afraid to now that the moment is here. What if I do and I lose him?

"Eric." He pokes me in the arm, much like Mattie does when she wants me to pay attention. We've all picked up her habits in one fashion or another.

"Will you just leave me alone?"

"No, I won't!" He shoves me this time, and I almost topple off the couch.

"Hey!" Once I've caught my balance, I glare up at him, only he's staring at me just as fiercely. I don't know what to make of his expression. "Look, I get it. If this is too weird for you…"

"You don't get anything. Who is this guy?"

"That's none of your damn business." Why is he so adamant about knowing?

Does he want to make sure to avoid him and me together or something? Little does he know that will be impossible.

"It is my damn business," he bites out. "Who?"

Standing, I take several steps away from him. "You don't want me to answer that question."

I feel him move until he's right behind me. His heat seeps into my back, he's so close. "I want to know."

Closing my eyes, I take a deep, shuddering breath. "I…I don't know if I can tell you that."

"You can, Eric. No matter what, you're always going to be my best friend."

Not after I tell him the truth, I won't.

"Is it that guy from our English Lit class last semester? The one who always sat next to you and tried to insert himself into our conversations?"

Laughter escapes. Chad. I can't even remember his last name. He wasn't gay. He was just a guy who loved football and thought it was cool he was friends with the wide receiver.

"It *is* him," Ethan says vehemently. "I

knew that idiot liked you."

Ethan sounds almost jealous.

"I don't like him," Ethan declares.

"You barely spoke to him. How do you know you don't like him?"

"Ah ha! I knew it. It *is* him!"

I turn and look at him, surprised. He sounds angry and jealous all at once.

"What is your problem with Chad?"

"He's a clinger. He tries too hard, and he's not good enough for you either."

"Uh…"

"Don't 'uh' me." Ethan points at me, and I back up, but he follows. "Do you even know that much about him other than he likes football?"

"Uhhh…"

"He could be a crap kisser for all you know."

"Umm…"

"Unless you've already kissed him?" Ethan's nostrils flare, and he gets even angrier.

"What is wrong with you?" I whisper.

"With me? I'm not the one going around kissing Clingy Chad. You're the one with the problem."

"If this is you freaking out because I told you about my liking guys…"

"No, it's not me freaking out over that. I don't care if you like men or women. You're my best friend, Eric. I'd never judge you for who you loved. Don't you know me better than that?"

"I was scared, man. After my granny died, I had no one. I'm afraid to lose all of you. That's why I didn't tell you. I can't lose you too."

Ethan runs a hand through his hair. "I can't lose you either."

"That won't happen, man. We're family."

"But you didn't trust me with this part of yourself."

"It's not like that."

"Then what's it like?" he demands, getting angry again. "Do Mattie and Mary know?"

"They figured it out even before I did."

Ethan sighs. "I must be blind, then."

Yeah, I've had that same thought. He has to see how I look at him sometimes. He can't not see it unless he doesn't want to.

"Look, we're cool. If you can deal with me…" I pause, searching for the right words but not finding them.

"Being gay?"

"I wouldn't call myself gay. I like women too much for that."

"Bi, then?"

"I don't know, honestly. Zeke and I have been talking it through. He says I don't need to label myself. To just be me and don't worry about the rest."

"It's sound advice."

"Yeah, it is. Anyway, as long as you're cool with me, then we'll still be friends."

"But you're thinking about going to go see Clingy Chad?"

"Ethan…"

"No."

"Look…"

"No, you're not going to see him."

I let out a pent-up laugh. "You can't tell me not see someone just because you don't like them."

"I don't want you seeing *any* guy."

My shoulders slump. He said he was okay with it, but maybe he's not. Maybe he was just saying that, trying to convince himself as much as me.

"I don't want you seeing *anyone*."

The last word was said with such displeasure, I glanced his way. He had that fierce look back on his face again.

"What are you talking about?"

"I mean it, Eric. The thought of you with someone, with anyone, it does something to me. If I lost you to some random guy or even a girl, I…" He stops and takes a deep breath. "You're not the only one who's been struggling with feelings they didn't ask for."

What's he saying?

"I don't understand."

"I swear, sometimes you're dense." Ethan shakes his head, and he gets this look I see sometimes when he's in hardcore gaming mode. It's like he's made up his mind about a course of action and will see it through even if he loses in the process. He tells me you can't learn if you don't take chances.

He stalks toward me, and I find myself backing up again until I hit the wall. He keeps coming and stops when the tips of his shoes bump mine. He's so close, it's claustrophobic.

"What are you doing?" I ask, alarmed.

"Something I should have done a long time ago, but I was too scared."

Ethan's hands come up and land on the wall on either side of my head, and he leans in.

"Ethan…"

"Be quiet."

My breath catches as he comes toward me until his lips press on mine. They're softer than I thought they'd be. That's the only thought I can grasp as a volley of sensations hit me all at once. I'm so shocked, all I can do is stand there, frozen.

He pulls back. "You know, this doesn't work right if you don't kiss me back."

"I…I…" I'm stuttering, but I can't help it.

Ethan laughs softly, one hand coming up to cup my cheek. His thumb strokes over my bottom lip. "I've been thinking about kissing you for months. I dream about it most nights, but I was scared, Eric. I've never had feelings for a guy before. I'm not going to lose you to

Clingy Chad because of my own fear."

He likes me the same way I like him? He was as scared as I've been about feeling this way?

I blink, trying to find words, but they won't come.

"When I said I understand, I meant it."

"I don't like Chad," I whisper, my voice barely audible.

He cocks his head. "You don't?"

"No. He was just a friend."

"Then who?" he demands, some of the anger coming back into his expression. "Because you don't need him."

"I don't?"

"No. You have me. That is…if you want me?"

If I want him?

"I was afraid…what if you thought I was a sick fu—"

"Shhh." Ethan shushes me with his finger on my bottom lip coming up to cover them both. "You're not sick. You're Eric."

My bottom lip quivers beneath the pressure of his finger, and all my fear and anxiety melt away in the tender fierceness of his expression.

"The only person I ever wanted was you." The words leave me in a rush.

"Me?" he whispers.

"I was so terrified you'd see how I felt about you then pissed you didn't see it when everyone else did. But mostly I was afraid you would, and you'd leave me."

"Leave you?" He smiles softly. "Why would I leave you, Eric? You're my best friend...no, you're my person."

"Your person?"

"You're my Christina, and I'm your Meredith. You're my person."

Someone's been binge watching *Grey's Anatomy*. But it's the sweetest thing anyone's ever said to me.

"Who says I'm Christina?"

Ethan laughs. "You're fearless. You rush in and save the people you love. Meredith is a little more cautious but just as insane. I'm like that. If I'd been more like Christina, then I'd have kissed you at Christmas."

I swallow thickly, unable to speak past the lump in my throat.

"So, how about this time when I kiss

you, you kiss me back, huh?"

"I…"

Another laugh from Ethan. "Don't you want to kiss me?"

I nod, not trusting my voice. I swear I feel like I'm back in junior high school, kissing my crush for the first time. My palms are all sweaty, and I'm trying desperately to remember if I had onions on the burger Mrs. Banks made for lunch. No one wants to kiss someone with onion breath…

"You're thinking too hard, Eric."

Yeah, probably.

When he comes in this time, I'm a little more prepared, and I kiss him back, putting all my feelings for him into that one kiss. It's like he's reached in and touched my soul with each stroke of his tongue against mine.

He pulls back, and we're both breathing heavier than we were. "That was…wow. I never knew you could kiss like that. I might have kissed you sooner if I'd known that."

I lean my forehead against his. "Thank you for being braver than me."

"I was going to lose you to Clingy Chad. I couldn't let that happen. You're more important to me than my fears and insecurities, Eric. You always will be."

Someone clears their throat behind us, and we both turn our heads to see Mary standing there, a huge smile spread across her face.

"Cass is here."

She doesn't comment on the way we're pressed against each other, which is a relief. This is new, and we both need to process it, but neither of us broke apart like we'd done something wrong either. I didn't even have the urge to do that and hurt Ethan in the process. I'll never hurt him as long as I live. I'll protect him with my dying breath.

"Ready to go upstairs?" Ethan asks.

I nod. "Yeah, let's go get our sister back."

Ethan takes my hand and pulls me along as we follow Mary upstairs. For the first time since Mattie disappeared, I feel a little bit of peace.

And that's all because of Ethan.

When we hit the stairs, my smile is just

as wide as Mary's.

Cass

New Orleans, LA

I'm so tired, all I want to do is curl up in my bed and sleep for de next week, but I can't do dat. I got a 911 text from Mary Cross. Emma Crane is in need of help. She's gone and gotten herself into some kind of trouble, and Mary needs my help to get her ou' of it. I'm no' sure what kind of trouble it is, but Em's helped me more times den I can count. She's saved my life just as many times too. De girl is freaking scary, but she's still my friend. No, she be family. Half-demon or no', she's my family.

My phone died a couple hours ago, so I'm no' sure if they've already taken care of de situation. Still, I dragged myself here after catching a ride from a hunter I knew. I had him drop me off at a diner and den called an Uber to bring me to de Crane estate. Hunters aren't too fond of de Cranes in general. And for good reason. Dey're bad people who do bad things.

Unless you're a Crane. I've seen how much Ezekiel Crane loves his daughter, how he's gone above and beyond to make sure she's safe. Dat is his one redeeming quality—his love for his family.

I t'ank de driver and climb out. Hopefully, Mary or Eric will have a charger I can use to charge my phone. Emma talked me into getting an iPhone just so we could FaceTime. De only downside is dat it doesn't have a universal charger. I had no idea my tires would blow out and I'd be stuck in Nowhereville overnight. Dey didn't have de tires I needed either. I called a friend of mine who's going to haul my car home on his wrecker. He owed me a favor, so at least I'm not out any money.

De door's ripped open before I can even knock. Nat'aniel Buchard, Emma's bro'der, glares at me. "What took you so long?"

"Tires blew out. I had to bum a ride and make sure my car landed back home."

Som'tin's very wrong. I can feel it as soon as Nat'aniel moves aside and I enter de house. It's like a shadow of darkness has descended upon it. I feel it in my bones.

Zeke and his parents are in de library when Nat'aniel ushers me in. Dey all appear haggard. Zeke glances up, and he has dis look in his eyes dat puts me on guard. I'm no' sure wha' it is, and I'm definitely sure I doan like it.

"Cass." Lila Crane comes over and hugs me. Stiffening, I try my best not to bark at her to back off. Dis be Emma's grandmo'der, and I won't be rude to her. She's been no'tin but nice to me since I've started coming around.

"What's going on?" I ask when she finally lets me go. "All Mary's text said was Emma was in trouble and she needed me to help." I make sure my Cajun accent is gone. I doan like usin' it around strangers, and I consider Nat'aniel a stranger.

"Didn't you get the rest of my texts?" Mary asks as she, Eric, and Ethan come t'rough de door. All our eyes zero in on de fact Ethan is holdin' tight to Eric's hand, who's blushin'. About time dose two stopped dancin' around each o'der.

"No, my phone died."

"Kristoff has Mattie, and we can't get to her."

"And none of your precious hunters will help us," Nat'aniel bites out. "After she's done nothing but try to help them."

As much as I'd like to say I'm surprised, I'm no'. Hunters doan trust de Crane name.

"How do you know he has her?"

"Because she snuck out of the house and handed herself over to him," Eric snarls.

"She did what?" My alarm spikes at

dis news. I swear dat girl doan know how no' to get herself in trouble.

"It was Mary's mother who forced the decision." Zeke stands and brings me Emma's phone. I look t'rough de text messages and photos of Mary's mother. Emma would never put Mrs. Cross in danger. She cares more about other people dan she does herself, which makes her a good hunter. But it also makes her vulnerable to t'rets like dis one.

But all her hunting skills woan help her now. Alice, my best friend, told me wha' Kristoff did to her, de head games he played wit' her while he fed from her. He's a sick, twisted psychopat'.

"This is bad."

"No shit, Sherlock," Nat'aniel mutters.

"Swear jar," Mary and Eric say automatically.

It's ano'der reminder dat Emma's no' here. I have dis awful feeling in de pit of my stomach dat's gettin' worse.

"Where's Dan?"

"He's…" Zeke breaks off and takes a deep breath. "Whatever is preventing us from getting a read on her is not affecting their bond. He's in a lot of pain."

"Which means so is she," I say slowly. Kristoff loves pain. He never physically hurt Alice, which is odd, considerin' all de damage he'd done to de o'ders. In her head, dou, dat was a different story altogether. He kept her in constant agony.

Zeke makes a sound, and I can see de pain on his face. He's hurtin' because his child is. Sometimes I wish I still had dat, but with both my parents gone, I doan.

"The witches from West Virginia are trying to find a way to break the spell over the crawlers in the water so we can get onto the island. But until they do, it's too dangerous for us try to breach it."

Mary twists her hands as she speaks. I've never seen her do dat before. She's tryin' to be calm, but she's no'. She's startin' to panic inside. Emma told me wha' she and Mary went t'rough at de hands of her old foster mo'der. Mary has to be havin' flashbacks t'inkin' of wha' Emma's going t'rough right now.

"What can I do to help?"

"Funny you should ask that, my darling boy."

My head whips around to see de demon Silas lounging against the fireplace. He hadn't been dere before. I know because I always make a sweep of every room I enter. It's som'tin Uncle Rob taught me when he was teachin' me and Robert to be hunters.

He's dressed in black slacks and a white dress shirt, his usual attire. The English accent is t'icker today, dou. I know he loves Emma in his own way and has gone above and beyond to keep her safe, but I doan trust him.

You never trust a demon. Ever.

It's de first rule of hunting.

"That's why we called you," Mary said. "You're the only person who can help."

"Me?"

"Your blood, more specifically."

"Silas has a spell. It's an old one, but it requires the blood of an angel, a demon, and a reaper. Basically, Heaven and Hell, with a binding force that can traverse both planes."

"And the bloodlines have to be related to the person you're scrying for."

"I doan understand."

"We've found out some information about your heritage. Silas was able to identify your mother's species." Mary takes a deep breath. "She was an Angel, one of the fallen."

"I am no' a Fallen Angel!" Dere is no way I have dat kind of evil in me. No way.

"No, you're not, my darling boy." Silas steps forward, coming closer, and I take an instinctive step back. I know he'd have no qualms about killin' me if it meant protectin' his granddaughter. "She's one of the fallen, not a Fallen Angel, who was cast out of Heaven by God himself after the great war with Lucifer. Your mother's kind decided to fall from grace on their own. In her case, it was because she fell in love with a mortal man."

Et'an shoves a chair at me as my knees buckle, and he barely gets it under me before I fall. I'm part Angel? I doan know wha' to say, how to react.

"And de man, he was my fa'der?"

"He was, but he didn't love her in

return, so she hid her pregnancy from him. She even lied to him later when he asked her if the boy was his."

Dis from Zeke. He looks pissed off now.

"You know who my fa'der is?"

"I do."

"Den who is it?" I whisper. It's a question dat has been hauntin' me since I found out I wasn't really a Willow.

He takes a deep breath. "It's me, Cass. I'm your father."

"No!" I stand, de chair falling backward. "You be lyin'. You're no' my fa'der. My mo'der wou' ne'ver…"

"He's not lying." Mary puts her hand on my arm. "I promise you, Cass, he's not."

I shake my head, refusin' to believe it. He's a Crane. I'm no' a Crane. I doan have demon blood in me. *I doan*.

"I know this is hard to hear, Cass."

"You know?" I shout at her.

Nathaniel growls and shoves her behind him. "Careful."

"Cass won't hurt me," Mary huffs and tries to step around him, but he sidesteps, keepin' her behind him. If I wasn't so upset, I'd be laughin', but bloody hell, dere's no way I'm a Crane.

"Cass," Zeke starts, but I put up a hand to stop him. I doan want to hear it. I want no'tin to do wit' him.

Unable to process, I turn and barrel past Nat'aniel, running blindly until I'm outside. Escaping into de maze of gardens, I find a spot hidden away from view and collapse to de ground.

It's hard to get air into my lungs, and I wheeze.

Dis has to be a panic attack.

I've heard about dem but never experienced one before.

No wonder Uncle Rob refused to tell me who my fa'der was. He hates de Cranes. He taught us to hate dem as well. He'd never willingly allow dem near me. He might be civil to Emma, but he'd ra'der we leave her to her own devices and stop askin' her for help.

Emma.

If dis be true, she's my sister.

My lungs shudder, and it's like breat'in' t'rough a straw.

My sister.

I might have a sister.

I'm no' a Crane.

I can't be.

But I have Zeke's eyes. De exact same shade of blue. I was about eight de first time I saw him, and I remember t'inkin' it was funny de tall man had my eyes. Uncle Rob flew mad and told me to never say dat again.

He scared me so bad at de time, I tried to hide whenever Ezekiel Crane was wi'tin sight. My uncle fostered dat fear and turned it into a burning hatred. No' just me ei'der, but in Robert and Caryle too.

And it's no' just de idea of being a Crane.

De t'ought of having demon blood runnin' t'rough my veins makes me physically ill. I've spent my entire life huntin' demons and o'der evil creatures. To be told I'm now evil? It's more dan I can handle. I doan want dis. I doan want any part of it.

Is dis how Emma felt when she learned de trut' about herself? I doan know how she came to terms wit' it, because I'm havin' a hard time.

But Emma's no' evil. She might get all dark and twisty when her demonic side comes out, but I've never seen her do any'tin evil. She tries so hard to help people. Even dose who doan want her help like de o'der hunters. No' one of dem lifted a finger to help find her.

And dat is no' fair.

I need to get myself toge'der and try to help get to her. She'd do it for me. Sister or no', she tol' me I was her family, and dat meant a lot to me. No matter wha' I'm feeling now, I have to put it aside and find Emma.

De scuff of shoes draws my attention from de patch of grass I'd been starin' at and directly to Ezekiel Crane. His blue eyes are stricken and so full of pain, I have no words for it.

He comes over and sits down in de grass in front of me. I doan want him here.

"It's a shock, I know." His deep voice is gruff. "When I found out, it floored me. Your mother told me point blank you weren't mine when I asked her. She had never lied to me before, so I trusted what she said. I'm sorry for that."

"She was protectin' me from you."

He nodded. "Yes, I think so too, but what she didn't realize is that I would have never harmed you because you were my son. I protect my family with everything I have."

"I doan want dis."

Ezekiel takes a deep breath. "I know you've been taught that I'm evil. Robert made no bones about how he felt about the Cranes. I won't lie to you, Cass. I'm not a nice person. I do bad things. But I love my family. And that includes you now. Whether you want my protection or not, you have it."

"I doan want to be evil," I whisper so softly I'm no' sure he even heard me until he speaks several heartbeats later.

"Is that what you think? That being a Crane makes you evil?"

I nod, unable to hide my fear from him.

"Because of the demon blood?" He lets out a sigh. "We were not even aware of it until Silas revealed to Emma Rose who he really was. We do not and will *never* willingly bed down with demons. I've used demons before, but to take one to bed? No. It is not what we do. The feelings you're having now are the same ones my parents and I suffered through. The same ones your sister had. We wanted no part of it either. We were disgusted to have it in our blood as well. Trust me, you are not the only one who has difficulties accepting that."

I am no' sure wha' to say. I t'ought for sure dey would love to have de power of a demon flowin' t'rough dem.

"Then we look at Emma. She is the kindest person I know under all that gruff exterior of hers. You've seen her at her best and at her worst. You tell me, do you think your sister is evil?"

I had just been t'inkin' about dis.

"No, Emma is no' evil. I know she has a dark side, but she fights it."

"She does," Ezekiel agrees. "I've seen her struggle with it. You've seen her demonic side. You know who she is, the whole truth. My daughter doesn't trust a lot of people. She hasn't even told

Nathaniel about her heritage, yet she told you. Why do you think that is, Cass?"

"Because de o'der hunters be askin' questions, and she knew she had to tell me de trut' if she wanted me to protect her."

"No, that's not why she told you the truth."

I cock my head questioningly.

"The only people who know the truth of who she is are in that house. The people she calls her family. She decided you were her family before she even found out you were her brother."

"She knows?"

"Yes. It all came out yesterday. I didn't know that your father wasn't your biological father until she revealed she and Dan were searching for the truth of your parentage."

He must have been shocked. He still looks like he's reelin' from de truth.

"I didn't know your mother was an Angel. Angelic blood prevents my gift from working."

"Wha' do you mean, your gift?"

He takes a deep breath. "The only

reason I am telling you this is because you're my son, and if I want you to trust me, then I have to trust you too."

Never happen.

"When I ask people direct questions, they can't lie to me. It's partly why I'm so successful. I've not done nearly as many bad things as you've been led to believe because I don't have to. People don't lie to me."

"Wha'?" I ask, horrified. No one in de huntin' community is aware of dis. If dey were, no one would come near de Cranes.

"It's a gift every member of my family has. It's how we manage to glean information without actually hurting anyone. I bet no one told you that, did they?"

No, no, dey hadn't. I'd been taught de Cranes used any means necessary to get wha' dey wanted.

"I also send hundreds of shipments of food, clothes, and medicine to third world countries each month so they don't starve. I have a charity that donates millions so children who otherwise couldn't afford the surgeries they need get them. I fund reading programs for children and adults around the country. I'm not as bad as you've been taught to believe, Cass. No one promotes the good things I do, only the bad."

I hadn't heard one single t'ing about any of dat.

"It still doan change de bad t'ings you do on de regular."

A hint of a smile ghosts across Zeke's face. "No, I suppose not, but at least you know I'm not all bad. Your mother saw the good in me, but I wasn't in love with her. She was a remarkable woman, though. I always respected and admired her. I was happy for her when she found someone who could love her the way she deserved."

"You said you didn't know she was an Angel?"

He shakes his head. "Not all people with supernatural abilities recognize each other despite what you see on TV or read in books. Your mother hid who she was well."

I file dat information away. It is some'tin hunters have debated about forever.

"My point is that I know this has to be hard for you. You're in shock. I understand. I'm in a little shock myself to have a full-grown son who probably hates the ground I walk upon."

I wince. He's no' wrong.

"But you *are* my son, and that matters to me. And to your grandparents, as you just witnessed. They are excited to have another grandchild to lavish affection upon. It took Emma Rose a while to warm up to them, so they're not expecting anything miraculous from you. Just understand they will love you even if you can't bring yourself to love them. All I ask is that you're civil to my parents."

"Dey always been civil to me, so I try to be civil to dem. Dat woan change."

"Good. I saw you stiffen up earlier, and I know how possessive Lila gets."

Emma has tol' me about dat. She's also convinced Lila's ashamed of her despite her grandmo'der's protests. If she's ashamed of Emma, she sure will be of me and my backwoods Cajun.

"I just hope after the shock has worn

off, you'll give us a chance to at least get to know one another. I think if you do, you'll find a family who will love you no matter what. We're Cranes. We take care of each other."

I'm no' sure I can do dat, but I doan say it out loud. The man is tryin'. I woan t'row it back in his face. Especially with his o'der child missin' and most likely bein' tortured.

"Tell me about dis spell de demon wants my blood for."

"As Mary said, it's ancient, predating most of the written word. It's also demonic."

"And you want me to let a demon use my blood in *a demonic spell*?" I can't keep de derision out of my voice.

"If it were for anyone except Emma Rose, I'd never ask you. I spent the better part of fifteen years searching for her, and to have her taken from me again…" His voice breaks, and I see de pain plain as day on his face. He's hurtin' in a bad, bad way. "I swear to you, Cass, I won't let Silas near your blood. I can cast it, or one of the witches from West Virginia.

Or you can do it yourself. This is for Emma Rose. She'd do it for you without a thought for herself."

He's right. Emma wou' and never t'ink of de consequences or how much it cost her personally. Dat be how she is. If you're family, dat's all she needs to know. She'd move mountains to get to me.

I'd never forgive myself if I didn't do de same for her.

"Fine. As long as de demon or Nat'aniel doan touch my blood."

"I swear to you they won't."

"How soon do you want to do dis?"

"Silas has gone searching for the last few things he needs, so probably not until tonight or tomorrow."

"Okay. Can I use your phone to call Rob to come get me? I need to sleep. I been up most of de night."

"You can use one of the rooms upstairs."

There's fear in his eyes, a fear if I leave now, I won't come back. And dat means Emma might die. I'd never do dat to her. But it's more den dat too. But I doan want to t'ink about dat right now.

"You can use Eric's room."

He sounds desperate, not dat I blame him. If it were my kid, I'd do ever'tin I could to get her back too.

"Okay, but I doan want dat demon popping in while I sleep."

"I wish I could promise that, but Silas has slipped past every demon ward I've ever put up. I will ask Eric and Ethan to go upstairs. Their rooms are directly across from each other. Leave the doors open, and they'll see if Silas sneaks into your room."

"I need to call Uncle Rob to let him know where I am."

"You can use the house phone."

Zeke stands and holds his hand out to me.

I doan want to take it.

But a small, almost forgotten part of myself whispers dat I do want to take his hand. I do want wha' I've missed since I was little.

Reaching up hesitantly, I latch onto de offered hand, and he pulls me up. Only he doesn't drop my hand like I expect him to. He pulls me into de tightest hug I've ever had. Not even Uncle Rob hugged me like dis when my parents died. I feel all de emotions Zeke is trying to keep under control, but he can't hide de one emotion coming off him in waves.

I'm sensitive to emotions. Always have been.

De strongest sense of love I've ever felt seeps into my bones, and it frightens me to de point I stiffen up. I doan want dis, but at de same time, dat little whisper calls me a liar. I miss havin' a family dat loves me more den any'tin else.

Not dat Uncle Rob doesn't.

He loves me.

But it's not de same love he feels for his own children.

I've always felt de difference, t'anks to dis hinky gift I have.

But Zeke? It's de same love I felt when my fa'der hugged me or kissed me when he put me to sleep at night. My fa'der loved me fiercely, but even dose feelings pale in comparison to Zeke's.

He finally pulls back, not upset I didn't hug him back.

"You're my son, Casstiel David Willow. I might have only found out about you yesterday, but that doesn't change how I feel. I've known you for months. I've grown to respect you during that time. You gave my daughter a chance when others spurned her. That meant a lot to me and your grandparents. Lila loved you the moment I told her. That's how she is. She loves fiercely and instantly. She's a lot like Emma Rose. As soon as she come to a determination about who she decides is family, that's it. She loves you for life."

"I love Emma too. She be my friend."

"She's your sister," he says quietly. "She was so happy and proud when she found out. I wish you could have seen her face."

I swallow past a lump in my throat.

"Come on. Let's get you inside so you can rest and get a shower. I'll have Eric give you some clean clothes. They might be a little big, but they should at least fit."

Eric is a football player, a wide receiver at dat. Dude's huge. "Uh, maybe

I'll ask Et'an. We're about de same size."

"Of course." Zeke nods. "Are you hungry? Mrs. Banks made her famous burgers. She has plenty left over."

"I wouldn't say no to food and a shower."

Zeke smiles, just as hesitant as I am. "Let's get you fed, then."

I follow him back inside, dis tightness in my chest. It's unfamiliar, and I scratch at it. I'm no' sure dis is a good idea, but I need to sleep, and at de same time, I want to ease some of de fear and worry in Zeke. He loves Emma. I love her too. She cou' be my sister. I'm still no' sure I believe dis, but I will do ever'tin in my power to save her. Not because of Zeke or anyone else.

But because she be my family. She chose me as her family before she even knew we migh' be related by blood. She was right den, and she's right now.

Sometimes de family you choose for yourself be more important den de family you're born into.

She chose me.

And I chose her.

Blood or no', I'll move de same mountains she wou' have for me to get her back.

Saidie

New Orleans, LA

I step out onto the back patio and look for Alesha, who had texted me to come find her. Aleric's already outside somewhere, basking in the sunlight. He missed it so much in the years he'd been a vampire. At least one of us is enjoying our stay in New Orleans.

Not seeing her, I go farther into the gardens, finally spotting Alex's mom in the gazebo, sitting cross-legged as she pours over a text that looks ancient.

"Hey, is there any news?"

Alesha shakes her head and waves me to sit down.

Sighing deeply, I do as she asks. Even though I don't know Emma Crane that well, I do know Kristoff, and he's crazy. God only knows what kind of torture he's putting her through. Aleric assured me the vampire doesn't get off on sexual assault. He prefers head games and straight-up physical torture. There's that much to be thankful for.

Cass Willow, the hunter who is fond of Emma, arrived yesterday, and Silas hasn't returned either. He's collecting the things he needs for his ancient spell. It will, in theory, transport them directly to Emma, bypassing the creatures in the swamp. Alesha isn't sure that it'll work, though, and has been focusing on her own version of the spell, this one probably not requiring as much dark magic as a demon spell would.

When she's done muttering whatever incantation she was doing, she finally looks up at me. She's tired. Really, really tired. She hasn't slept much either. I've seen her at all hours of the day and night.

Alex and I have a theory. We're fairly certain Ezekiel Crane is her true mate. Which is all kinds of messed up. He's got a girlfriend who he seems to truly love, and she him. It's a hell of a mess if that's the case. We're both thinking Alesha is working herself to death to save his daughter because of the whole mate bond thing.

Jason and Alex are not sure how to feel about the thought of their mother mating with one of the most well-known criminals in the country. One the law has never been able to touch. And it's not just regular crime either. He's known as a very bad man in paranormal circles as well. Alesha would be damn stupid if she's not careful here. He could potentially hurt her very badly, mate bond or not.

"Have you slept at all?"

"Some," she says. "This spell requires a lot of work at different times. I need to be awake to complete all the moving parts."

"You should get some rest, Alesha. You're not going to do anyone any good if you're passed out cold."

She laughs. "I can go days without sleep and weeks living on an hour or two. Witches' blood and all that."

"So, like, a normal witch doesn't need sleep?"

"Yes, they do."

We both jump at the sound of Ezekiel's voice. He's standing just to the side of us. Neither of us heard him approach. He's like a cat. Just springs himself on you with no thought to the heart attack he's about to cause.

"But Ms. Blackburne is not a normal witch." He moves closer, and I'm struck at just how much he looks like that actor who played Ichabod Crane in that remake of *Sleepy Hollow* Fox did several years ago. It's uncanny and hella freaky.

"What do you mean?" I ask after a moment when it's obvious neither of them is going to elaborate.

"The Blackburnes are one of the three magical Families of Power in the paranormal community. And they're the most powerful of the three. Hence why there is a kill-on-sight order for her children. People are afraid of what they don't know. But with Alesha, there's more than just her family bloodline."

"You've done your homework," she murmurs.

"When it comes to the safety of my children, yes, Ms. Blackburne, I do my homework."

"Are either of you going to tell me what that means?"

"It means I've dealt more in black magic over the years than most."

"So? You always say true magic is neither good nor bad, it's a combination of the two. Why does it matter how much you do of one kind of magic over the other?"

"It matters because when a witch performs magic, our soul is used as a catalyst of sorts. When we do black magic, it leaves a stain on our soul. It's how witches go dark."

Oh… "Hell."

"Pretty much," Alesha says, laughing. "If not for Alex and Jason, I probably would have gone dark a long time ago. They've kept me from becoming my father."

"Speaking of your father, do you wish to travel to your family plantation home here in New Orleans? It's not far from here, and I can arrange to have someone take you."

"I'm surprised you didn't suggest we stay there."

"I can't keep you safe there. Here, I know my wards. It's all but impenetrable."

Alesha cocks her head in question.

"Silas." Ezekiel grimaces. "That demon has gotten through every demonic ward that's ever been built."

"He's quite slippery."

"You know him?"

Alesha nods. "We've crossed paths once before. It was after the memory spell I did on Emma when she was little. He wanted to know where she and her mother were. I could honestly answer I didn't know." A sly smile flits across her face. "He learned very quickly not to try to intimidate me. I don't deal with threats very well."

"You sound a lot like my daughter.

She's fearless."

"As is my daughter. Alex had a rough life, but it didn't break her. She's fearless in her own right."

Not exactly true, but close enough. Her grandfather broke her, and she's healing from the mind games he played with her. I don't know if she'll ever really come back from it, but if Alesha wants to believe she will, I'm not going to tell her otherwise.

"Emma was taken from us when she was two and later put into the foster care system. I didn't find her until she was seventeen. She learned to survive on her own. It's what I'm counting on to keep her safe until we can get to her." He gestures to the mess she has going on around us. "I'm assuming this is part of finding her?"

"This is part of getting onto the island." Alesha turns her attention to me. "Give me your hand."

I do it without question, even when she brings out a small knife. I'm assuming it's silver. That seems to be the blade of choice amongst paranormal magic wielders, at least in my limited understanding of it. A witch, I am not.

Ezekiel snatches my hand away from Alesha before she can even get the blade near my flesh. "What do you think you're doing?"

"I'm finishing my spell."

"With her blood?"

"It's necessary."

He turns his attention to me. "Never, ever let anyone have your blood. It is the single most powerful element in all of magic. It can be used against you."

"But Alesha's not going to do that." I gently take my hand back from him. "She won't hurt me."

"How do you know that?"

"Because if she did, Alex would never forgive her."

He frowns but doesn't move to retake my hand.

"I'm not a monster." Alesha actually looks hurt, and I feel bad for her. She knows this is her mate, a mate she stands zero chance of claiming as long as his girlfriend is in the picture.

"I'm a monster." Ezekiel sinks to the

ground beside us. "There's no harm or shame in admitting that. It keeps us alive when others die."

Her eyes flash up to him. "What if I don't want to be a monster?"

"I think that ship's already sailed, Ms. Blackburne."

Again, a look of hurt flickers through her eyes.

"So, what is this spell supposed to do?" It's probably best to get them the hell away from this line of conversation.

"The crawlers are spell bound to Kristoff's blood. It's the only way to ensure they ignore the call of a Necromancer. Mr. Crane was right about the blood being the single most powerful element in magic."

"Okay, so what does my blood have to do with breaking the spell if they're programmed to ignore my call?"

"Because Kristoff doesn't know what Madame knew." A very, very evil smile graces Alesha's lips, and it makes me slightly worried about this whole black stain on the soul thing. "Not only are your powers at their most wild right now, you're also the single most powerful Necromancer alive."

"What?" I whisper.

"Saidie, you're descended from the original Necromancer. You are the spitting image of her. And from the tests I've done, you've inherited all her abilities. You just don't know how to use them, or maybe unlock them might be a better way to put it. The crawlers, Kristoff, any dead thing, really, cannot ignore your call if you learn to harness your abilities."

"So, if I knew what I was doing, we'd already be on the island and be able to rescue Emma?" Dammit. I knew ignoring this curse was going to cost me more than acknowledging it. I don't want anyone to get hurt because of me.

But haven't all those poor women been hurt because I was afraid to come back here and face what I left? To face Kristoff?

"You can't look at it like that, young lady." Ezekiel takes my hand. He has calluses on his. I don't know why I'm so surprised by that. He looks like someone who never gets their hands dirty, but I know he does. Sabien gave us all a rundown on the Cranes.

"How am I supposed to look at it, then?"

"From my intel, this gift is something you've come into within the last two years. When that happens, it can be jarring not only to the system, but to the psyche as well. It takes time to come to terms with what that means. Time to adjust to the new reality you've been dropped into. Don't punish yourself because of it."

"You sound like you know something about it."

"I do." He gives me this crooked smile that is very charming. "I'm what's called a living reaper. I drowned when I was boy, and when I was resuscitated, my gift woke up. It's quite strange to start seeing the ghosts of the dead when you're only a child. So, yes, Saidie, I know something about it."

"When did it stop being strange?"

"Never. You just learn to live with it and hope you can use it to do some good."

"Have you managed it?"

He nods. "Yes. They come to me, and I help them move on, and in some cases, I've been able to get justice for them."

"Justice?"

"That's where part of my reputation comes from. I've dealt with a few situations where the only way to get justice was to land on the far side of the law."

"You do bad things for a good reason?"

"Sometimes. Other times, I do them for my own personal gain. Or just because I want to." His smile is as evil as Alesha's was earlier. "Never be afraid to admit who you are, Saidie. Hiding from yourself is far worse than hiding who you are from the world. That is how you truly go dark. The only way to combat the growing darkness inside you is to surround yourself with people who will constantly remind you of your humanity."

"You really believe that?"

"I do." He gives me what I presume is

his most charming smile. "Now, before I allow your blood to be used by a witch for any reason, I need to know more. You're my daughter's age, and there's nothing I can do to help her right now, but I can help you."

"That's…nice of you."

"I have my moments, *chèrie*." He turns his attention back to Alesha, and the frown reappears. "I will not allow her blood to be used unless there is no other way."

"I've consulted every witch I know, and the only way to break that spell is with our own blood bound spell, a more powerful one. One that will require me to help Saidie focus her gifts through a blood tie. So, yes, Mr. Crane, I need her blood, or this won't work, and we won't be able to breach the island."

"Why can't we breach it, though? I can have a helicopter drop us down. I've been giving this a lot of thought. The hunters have been trying to go in the same way you are right now."

"That's because it's Madame's island."

"You say that like it should mean

something to me."

"You didn't know who you had in your own back yard, Mr. Crane?" Alesha tilts her head curiously. "Considering you've proclaimed to do your own homework, I'm surprised."

"I know who she was, but I never had a reason to call upon her services or deal with her in any other capacity."

"I think it would be best for Aleric to be here. He actually grew up there, so he knows it better than any of us."

"That's an excellent idea."

I shoot him off a quick text to meet us here and study Alesha and Ezekiel. They're bristling at each other like two dogs circling a bone. It reminds me a little of the way Aleric and I fought. It also gives me hope that Alesha's still got a chance with Ezekiel.

"Mr. Crane…"

"Please, call me Zeke. My father is the only one who responds to Mr. Crane."

"Zeke." I like it a lot better than Ezekiel. Makes him less stuffy.

"My mother hates it, and that may be why I like it so much."

A shadow falls over us, and I know without looking it's Aleric. I feel him in my bones.

"Wha' is all dis?" He gestures to mess Alesha has spread out over the floor of the gazebo.

"Alesha's spell to get us past the crawlers."

He visibly shudders.

"You know the creatures well?" Zeke asks.

Aleric scoops me up and takes my seat, settling me in his lap. His body is tense, but so's mine. Talking about that place does it every single time.

"*Oui, Monsieur* Crane. It was Madame's favorite form of punishment for her children."

"And you were her son?"

"No' by choice, dou. She took me from my family when I was but a boy."

"I'm sorry."

Aleric shrugs. "It brou' me Saidie. I cain't be sorry for dat, sir."

"I suppose not." Zeke clears his throat. "These two are telling me I can't just drop in with a helicopter."

Aleric laughs, the sound harsh in the quiet peacefulness of the garden. "You wou' be dead before your feet touch de ground, sir."

"Explain."

"Madame was no' just a Necromancer, she was a witch as well. A very skilled witch. She used dat to her advantage. Dere are wards along ever' inch of dat island. She planned for it all. Invasion from land, invasion from de water, invasion from above. Each ward would have to be deactivated in de proper order, startin' wit' de crawlers. Dey be her first line of defense. Den comes de dead crawlin' all over de island. And dose, as many as dey are, dey doan even come close to de t'ings she created. The curses she put into place, like de one associated wit' an assault from above. Your insides wou' turn to mush, and you'd die a painful deat'."

"That sounds decidedly unpleasant."

"Pray you never find out, *Monsieur*."

"Can you remember all the wards?"

"I was no' privy to Madam's spellcrafting. We were tol' of dem, but dat's all I can tell you."

"Did you ever see any of them activate, besides the crawlers?"

"*Oui.*" A full body shudder rolls through him that doesn't escape either Zeke or Alesha. "Dey are terrifyin' to behold."

"Can you sit down and write out the ones you remember? Any little thing will help us."

"I'll have Saidie write dem out. I cain't read or write so well."

Zeke blinks. "I just assumed…you speak such good English…"

"Dere was a slave boy who taught me how to speak English. I only spoke Romani when Madame took me. De boy…he t'ought dat by helping me learn English, Madame, she wou' be grateful. I t'ought she was, but when my English improved to de point she understood me, she had de boy killed in front of me and his family. His kindness was repaid in blood. Dat be who Madame was, who you will be dealin' wit' on dat island. Dead she migh' be, but all her creations? Dey be dere, waitin' for anyone to come and t'reaten our home."

My heart shatters for him. How could someone do such a horrible thing and make Aleric watch it at such a young age? I'm so glad she's dead. If I could kill her again, I would just for this.

"I'll teach you to read and write."

"I can in Romani. My fa'der, he insisted we learn both Romani and Italian. It's just English dat I have problems wit'."

"Don't worry, we'll get you there."

"I have many, many books in my library that might help as well. You are welcome to use any of them."

Zeke isn't nearly as bad as I'd first thought he was. Then again, we're the only people trying to find his daughter. It gives him a reason to be super nice to us.

"That's very kind of you," Alesha murmurs. I'm not sure she means it, though. Witches think of Gypsies as slaves, and Alesha, nice or not, has those same preconceived ideas about Aleric's people. Racism exists everywhere, it seems, even in the supernatural world. Alex threatened to cut Alesha out of her life if she didn't accept Luka. Her mom's working on it.

Zeke stands. "The sooner you can get me the information, the better. I have people coming today who will be able to help."

"People?" Alesha asks.

"James Malone and his family. James is Dan's biological father, and he loves Emma Rose as much as Dan does. They're the only hunters besides Cass willing to help locate my daughter."

"I've dealt with James and his unit in the FBI over the years. He's good people."

Zeke doesn't agree or disagree, just tips his head our way and takes his leave.

Considering Ezekiel Crane is a criminal, I'm guessing the thought of having an FBI agent in his home is not sitting well with him.

"Come, *Draga*, we will go put toge'der dis list for *Monsieur* Crane." Aleric stands with me in his arms and starts toward the path leading to the back deck. I barely have a moment to shout good-bye to Alesha before he's inside and taking the back stairs to our room.

He's upset, and there's only one thing that's going to relax him enough to get through the next few hours. One thing I am more than happy to help him out with.

He kicks the room door shut and lets me slide down his body as he reaches behind him and locks the door.

Yes, I am more than happy to help him relax.

Emma Rose

Fulsome Sanitarium, MO

The door creaks open, and I look up to see the ghoul who is loyal to Kristoff come in, carrying a McDonald's bag and a drink. He sets it on the floor then picks up the bucket I've been using to relieve myself in. He looks disgusted, but hey, that's not my fault. They are the ones who have me here. I'm not squatting on the floor if something's been provided for me.

"You need to eat." He kicks the bag to me, unwilling to come any closer. I try to remember if I'd hurt him at some point, but everything is blurred together. I'm not even sure how long I've been here, honestly. It could be hours, days, or weeks.

And I know it's Kristoff doing this. He wants me off my game.

Eli comes up behind me, his heat pressed against me. I take comfort in his presence. He hasn't left since he showed up. He promised not to, and so far, he's kept that promise.

"I'm not hungry." I'm starving, actually, but for once my stomach doesn't give me away by growling.

"I don't care if you are or not. The more blood Kristoff takes from you, the weaker you're going to be. He wants to keep you around for a few more days. If you don't eat, you die, and I'd rather keep my head, thank you."

So, he's been charged with keeping me alive. Good to know.

When I don't move to pick up the bag, he gives me a look meant to make me cower. Only it's not in me to cower to him. He doesn't scare me. He's only a lackey.

"I will shove that burger down your throat."

"You can try."

He smiles, and it's not at all nice. "Oh, I'll do more than try, little girl. Don't test me."

"You won't kill me."

"No, I won't, but that doesn't mean I won't hurt you."

"I guarantee I'll hurt you more."

He shakes his head and comes at me. I'm ready for him, though. When his hands reach for me, I duck and sweep my leg at him, hitting him squarely in the knee. It's the one spot I know that will take down the biggest opponent. Eric taught me that, and Dan reinforced it.

I'm faster than he is, and when he drops, I'm behind him, and his arm is pulled up in the most painful hold I can manage. He struggles, but I yank it up tighter. A distinct crack sounds, and he screams.

I broke his arm.

Holy fudgepops.

I broke his arm.

How did I do that?

"Bravo, pet, bravo."

I go completely still at the sound of that voice. The voice that scares me worse than anyone or anything.

"He's not worse than Deleriel." Eli's whispered words pull me out of the rabbit hole I'd been perilously close to falling into. *"Don't show him any fear. He feeds off it. Be strong, Hilda. I'm right here with you."*

No, Kristoff isn't Deleriel, but he's close. It's those ice blue eyes of his that cause me the most dread. They're the eyes of a deranged psychopath. One whose sole purpose is to hurt me.

But Eli's right. Fear only feeds the monster.

"I told him not to test you, pet." Kristoff picks up the McDonald's bag. "Let him loose."

I drop his arm and take an instinctive step back. Kristoff tosses the bag to me.

"But he is right. You need to eat if you're going to get through the games I have planned for you tonight. You'll need your wits about you."

"Games?"

"Mmmm." He reaches down and pulls the ghoul up, inspecting the quickly swelling arm. "It's a clean break. It should heal in a day or two."

"Can I…will you…" The ghoul licks his lips, and I turn away, disgusted.

"No," Kristoff snaps. "You brought this on yourself. I told you to leave her alone. You know how dangerous she is, even in her limited state."

Another fact I file away. I may not have access to my gifts, but apparently my strength is still there. I've only ever accessed this type of strength when my demonic side comes out. Interesting.

I sit down on my mattress and open the bag. A Big Mac and three of those little double cheeseburgers are inside. I am hungry, and I feel woozy. Food will help me with that. It's been a few days since I ate last, I think.

"Eat, Hilda. You need it."

I unwrap the first little burger and bite into it. Tastes okay. It's not long before I'm devouring the second one. Kristoff hands me the Coke, and I drink it down greedily.

"There's something different about you." Kristoff sits beside me, his eyes assessing. "What is it?"

I shrug. I'm not telling him my Guardian Angel is on my other side. He'd probably find a way to make Eli go away.

"You seem calmer, more confident."

"I remembered something."

"What is that, pet?"

"I survived a Fallen Angel."

"You did. I was very impressed."

"You're not worse than he was. I survived him, and I'll survive you."

"There's one difference. You had all your abilities then. You don't now."

"I survived worse than you growing up, and I didn't have my abilities then either."

"Ah, yes, the poor, unloved little foster girl." He strokes my hair, and I fight back a flinch as I open the Big Mac box. "Perhaps I chose wrong."

I cut my eyes to him in question.

"Perhaps I should have made you my human servant." He cups my cheek and turns me to face him. His eyes are piercing.

"You have one?"

He nods. "Aye. My little hunter became my human servant. As long as she's out there, I can't die."

I swallow. He's talking about Alice. Cass's best friend Alice. Holy fudgepops.

"And if you die, does that mean she does as well?"

"Of course. She's a witch, but she'd need stronger blood than that to survive my death. I did make her harder to hurt, but when our bond breaks, so will she."

"So, if I kill you, I'm killing Cass's best friend." I say it more to myself than to him. Cass will never forgive me if I do that, but what choice do I have? I can't let Kristoff survive. He has to be destroyed.

"Ah, yes, I'd forgotten that." Kristoff's elongated fingernails bite into the flesh of my cheek, but I don't make a noise. Eli gives me strength and power. Having him here is making me braver.

I shove more food into my mouth.

"Something is definitely different with you."

Without warning, he lunges, and I'm on my stomach with him covering me. I try to buck him off, but even with my new strength, he's still stronger than I am.

His teeth sink into the flesh of my shoulder, right where the vein runs below the collar I'm wearing.

It hurts like nobody's business, but I don't say a word. Eli's hand finds mine and squeezes. I focus on that instead of the pain rampaging through my body. His heat seeps into me, and I close my eyes. I love the furnace that is Eli Malone.

Kristoff growls and shoves up, dragging me with him. "What are you playing at, pet?"

"I'm not playing at anything, Kristoff. I told you I realized tonight that you're not a Fallen Angel. I'll survive you."

"You think so?" His fingernails bite into my arms where he holds me.

"I know so." I grin, my grin that I haven't used in years. The one full of teeth and the promise of pain. Without even thinking about it, I bring my forehead forward with as much force as I can and smash it into his face. Bones crunch, and he grunts, but he doesn't let go.

"I like this you better."

He stands, his hand gripping me by my hair, and drags me out of the room.

No, no, no, no!

The insane ghosts are out here.

He tosses me down the hall. A good chunk of my hair is in his hand when I push up off the floor.

"Perhaps I don't scare you, pet, but I know what does. Don't ever forget I know every fear you have."

"I *will* kill you."

"What would Cass say about that, though, pet? You'll have murdered his best friend."

"He's a hunter. Both of them are. They'd understand."

"Are you sure?"

"Yes." I'm not, though. Cass probably wouldn't ever forgive me.

He laughs and comes forward. "What did I say, Mattie Louise? What keeps your loved ones safe?"

"My loved ones are safe. Zeke will

have them all at his house, and you're not getting past his security."

"Not all of them are there. How about this young lady?"

Kristoff pulls out his phone and swipes a few times before showing it to me.

No.

"You lay a hand on Ava, and I don't care who hates me. I'll kill you where you stand."

"Ah-ah, little one. The rules are simple. Do as you're told, and your family doesn't die. Keep defying me, and young Ava meets the same fate as all the others. The same fate you're going to meet when I grow bored of you."

Eli is stiff as a board as he stares at his sister. The time stamp is in real time. Wherever Ava Malone is, Kristoff has eyes on her.

I spit in his face.

He backhands me.

I spit out blood.

"Are you done yet?" he asks.

"Don't touch her."

He hits me so hard I stagger back and fall to the ground. Kristoff follows me and pulls out a knife. It's the same kind of knife my mother used to stab me. An exact replica.

It cuts into the flesh right below my wrist and travels up until it hits the top of my shoulder. He pulls me up and licks the blood welling out of the wound.

"You taste like my mum's cherry tart." He sucks at the wound when it stops bleeding, using his teeth to tear it open. "So sweet."

"You won't touch her," I repeat.

"I'll do whatever the hell I want, pet. I may even let my ghoul spend a few hours with you tied to the bed. I don't have those urges anymore, but he does. As I said before, don't test me, because you won't win."

"You do that, and I'll kill him."

He smiles. "He can't die."

"Try me. I found a way to destroy a Fallen Angel and a primordial evil, the same type of demon responsible for your existence. What's a ghoul compared to them?"

I may sound brave, but inside I'm quaking, shattering. I do not want to get raped, but the truth is Kristoff could make me lie there and let his ghoul do whatever he wanted, and I wouldn't be able to stop him.

Kristoff sighs. "I believe you would, and I've put too much time into him to lose him now. It takes time to train a good ghoul."

Relief hits swift and hard.

"That doesn't mean I won't, though. If you keep trying to defy me, I will give you to him while I let your blood rebuild. He's known for rough sex and mutilation. Knives are a favorite of his."

He knows how much I hate knives, but more than that, he knows how much they scare me. When I get out of this, I am going to overcome that fear. Knives will never paralyze me again.

"I've already told you the consequences of that, Kristoff. Test me, and you'll find out how far *I'll* go as well. I'm here. I'm playing your games. If you keep threatening the people I love, then you and I are going to have a serious problem."

He laughs, a full-on belly laugh, and it

irritates me like nothing else he's done. He thinks it's funny that I'm trapped here, threatening him, when he knows this danged collar prevents me from following through on any of my own threats. I thought I knew hate, but the truth is, I didn't. Until now. Now I understand the difference between rage and hate. Deleriel was rage, and Kristoff is hate.

"You are such a treasure, Mattie Louise Hathaway."

"My name is Emma Crane."

His smile is almost kind. "Deep down, you are and will always be Mattie Louise Hathaway. You know that, pet."

Maybe I do, but I don't want to be Mattie Louise Hathaway anymore. She spent most of her life being alone, having no one who cared about her, and living in fear. Emma Crane is brave, and people love her. I thought for a long time I could merge the two, but I'm not so sure now. Eli's telling me I have to be Mattie. Kristoff says I am Mattie, but I don't know who I am.

And that's the problem.

When my soul was shattered, I lost a part of myself. Or the parts didn't fit back together so well anymore. I'm not sure which. I've been lying to myself since then, pretending I'm fine, but I'm not. Not really. I'm not whole. I'm floundering…

"Stop it, Hilda."

Eli's whisper breaks through my fog of self-doubt, but it's not enough to pull me out of it. Because deep down, I do think I'm not worthy of being Emma Crane. Lila's embarrassed of me, my father, well, he loves me despite myself, and I'm embarrassed of me. I can't go to a function without doing something stupid. Mary should have been Lila's granddaughter. She's more high society than I am. She fits in better. She doesn't embarrass the Crane name.

"Snap out of it." Eli grabs me and shakes me hard. *"He's in your head. He knows every thought you've had, all your fears and doubts. He's using that against you right now. You are* not *weak. You're a fighter, Hilda. Now, stop wallowing and fight back. Fight him, or he'll kill*

you sooner rather than later."

I know he's going to kill me. It's inevitable.

"If you die, Dan dies. Are you prepared to be responsible for my brother's death?"

Dan.

Blinking, I come out of whatever fog I've been in. There is no force on Earth that will ever cause me to harm Dan. He's the reason I'm still breathing. He's my heart and soul.

The cold has creeped in around me during my moment of self-doubt and self-depreciation. The insane ghosts are everywhere. Even if I don't have access to my reaping abilities, I can still feel them around me. It's an innate ability that Kristoff can't take from me or suppress. It's who I am.

"That took less time than I thought, pet. You're very good at getting around me. It makes this all the more fun."

Kristoff creeps closer, his smile more wolfish. I give him one right back that is just as mean and ornery. Eli's right. I have to fight. I have to stay alive to keep

Dan alive.

"Can't he hear you?" I ask internally.

"No, Hilda. You're the only one who can hear me. I already told you that."

"What's this?" Kristoff comes closer and sniffs me. "Your mind is closed to me."

"Can you feel them?" I whisper when he gets so close, I can smell the death and decay coming off him.

"Feel what pet?"

"The ghosts. They're all around us, waiting for us to blink."

"To blink?" He squats in front of me.

"The ghosts down here were the most insane of them all. They've gone vengeful. Which means they can hurt you. Physically hurt you."

"They can't touch me."

"That's what you think." I cast my eyes to the left and then to the right. Even though I can't see them, I can still feel the cold. I can feel their anger and their rage. They want to hurt us as much as they're hurting.

"Ghosts are creatures of energy. They focus their energy enough, and you'd be surprised at what they can do. Some are tricksters, tripping you as you walk. Others are more dangerous, throwing things at you, sharp things that will slice through you. Some are so mad they've become almost physical creatures again. Those are the really dangerous ones. They could pick up a blade and slice your head from your neck before you even realized what was happening. Ghosts are not what you think they are, Kristoff. They're so much more."

His icy eyes are unreadable, but I know I made him flinch. I can smell the waft of fear coming off him.

"How can you feel them?" he asks after a moment. "I took your reaping abilities away from you."

"You took away my ability to *see* them, but I'm a living reaper, Kristoff. You can't take away what is ingrained in every fiber of my being. The cold seeps into my bones when they're near, and there's ones standing right beside you. His energy is angrier than most. There's something about you that's hitting a memory in him. Perhaps a doctor who you resemble hurt him or even took his life. Doesn't matter, I guess. You should be careful, though. He's one who can take your head."

"Enough!" Kristoff stands, bringing me with him. "I know what you're trying to do, Mathilda Louise, and it's not going to work."

"I'm not trying to do anything. I'm just telling you what's in front of you. It's up to you what you do with that information."

"No one is better at head games than I am, pet. Trying to fool the master of games is a definite no-no." His hand tightens around my upper arm until I hear the snap of a bone, but I don't cry out. I won't give him the pleasure of my pain.

"No one's better at pain than I am, Kristoff. You won't break me."

"Perhaps not, but I'll come damn close before I drain you dry, pet."

With that, he drags me back into my iron prison, his teeth sinking deep into the flesh of my shoulder until darkness blinds me.

"Come on, Mattie. We need to find shoes."

Shoes? I don't want to find freaking shoes. I want to go sit down and rest my feet. Meg has dragged me from one end of this mall to the other. And my feet freaking hurt.

"Can we eat first?"

She laughs, the sound bubbly, just like her. Throwing her heavy mane of blonde hair over one shoulder, she shakes her head. "You and your bottomless pit of a stomach. Fine, we'll take five to feed you, and then we have to check out that little boutique that just opened. They have shoes to die for."

"Right." I can't keep the snarl out of my voice. I don't want to be here. But I made a promise. If Dan lived, I'd try to be friends with the little backstabber who used to be my bestie. I'm trying, but my resolve is weakening.

She's acting like nothing ever happened, like she didn't betray me. Like she didn't violate not only the best friend code, but the most basic girl code. Don't mess with a guy you know your friend likes. I'm far from perfect, but that's something I would never have done to her. She's the worst BFF ever.

It actually hurts that she went and hooked up with Dan behind my back. Pain morphs into anger, but I beat it back. I promised to try. I keep my promises.

I want a burger, but she wants salad. We compromise with Chick-Fil-A. They have awesome chicken nuggets. Much better than McDonald's. Not that I'd ever turn down some Mickey D nuggets. I'm not overly picky with my food. Unless it's something that just sounds or looks nasty. Then I won't touch it no matter how yummy it smells. Gross is gross.

"Mattie, I wanted to say I'm sorry."
She puts her drink down on the table and looks me in the eye. "Neither Dan nor I wanted you to find out like you did. We'd planned to tell you after your birthday trip."

Really? Then why did Dan almost kiss me outside the restaurant? I want to snark that right in her innocent-looking little face, but I don't. Brownie points to me.

"It's not something we planned on. It's just that we spent so much time together with you while you were in the hospital, and then we'd go grab a bite to eat and talk..."

She trails off, and I can't stop the snarl from coming out. "Don't, Megan. If you want me to get to a point where I can have a civil conversation with you, then don't."

"I'm only trying to explain..."

"I don't want to hear it!" I shout then close my eyes, trying to regain control of my temper. I just want to go home and have this day be over.

"Mattie..."

I shake my head mutely. "Meg, what you did violated every code ever created between girls. I don't care if you were madly in love with him. What you did was wrong. That is not something I will ever forgive or forget. I will do my best to be civil to you because I promised if he lived, I'd try. That's all you're going to get from me right now. If you keep talking about it, you might end up with more than a broken nose."

She's quiet for a heartbeat, and when those blue eyes hit me, I flinch at the pain in them. "Is that why you killed me, Mattie? Were you so angry about me and Dan that you had to get me out of the picture?"

"I didn't kill you. Jake's brother did."

"Yes, but if you weren't there, he'd have never targeted me, now, would he?"

"I...what are you talking about?"

"You and I were friends. You hooked up with Jake, and that's how his brother found me. If Paul and I hadn't crossed paths through you and Jake, I'd still be alive. My death is your fault."

"You're wrong. We never hung out with Paul. I only met him once. He didn't meet you through me."

"But my death is your fault. Yours and Dan's. Can you deny that?" Her tone turns accusatory. "You chose each other over everyone, knowing there were consequences. He lived, and I went to that damn party. If he'd died, we'd have both been home grieving, and Paul wouldn't have had a chance to kill me."

I shake my head and blink. We aren't in the mall anymore. We're in the woods. The woods surrounding Lake Norman where Meg died. No. I can't be here.

Jake's lifeless body lies to my left, and a gunshot reverberates around me. Jake's staring at me, a gaping hole in his chest. His mouth is open, his brown eyes blown, and all he can do is silently scream. He points to me, and I know he's blaming me. His death is on me just as much as Eli's is.

"Mattie..."

I know that voice. Slowly, I turn and see a line of dead girls coming for me. They're all bloated from being in the water. These are the girls Mason drowned and whispered my name into their ears as he murdered them. They blame me for their deaths.

Branches break, and Meg appears in her beautiful ball gown, only it's covered in blood where the bullet went in and the wound bloomed. She hates me. I did this to her. My choice to beg him to come back to me, to stay for me. I killed her.

"I'm sorry," I whisper. "I never wanted anyone to die."

"You're selfish," she snarls, getting right up in my face. "You don't care about anyone but yourself. You never have. You're damaged goods, Mattie Hathaway. You don't deserve to be happy. You don't deserve to live when we all died because of you!"

Her hands wrap around my neck and start to choke me. Fingers dig into my hair as the other ghosts converge on me, and I desperately try to throw them off, but they have too tight a hold on me.

"You should be dead, not us," the drowned girl whispers in her broken voice. "If it wasn't for you, we'd all be

here. We'd have gone to prom, graduated, went to college. You have our life, and it's not yours. You need to die, Mattie Hathaway. Die like you should have all those years ago."

I should *have died when my mother stabbed me. If I'd just stayed dead, none of this would be happening. Dan would be safe.*

The fingers tighten around my throat.

"I told you, pet, you can't beat me at head games." Kristoff's words sink in, and just like that, I'm back in my dungeon, his lips attached to my wrist as he bleeds me nearly dry. He's stronger than I am when he's drinking from me.

"That's why you have to be the old Mattie," Eli says and curls around my body. *"You have to be cold, Hilda. You have to cut off your emotions. That's how he's getting to you. He's using your feelings against you."*

Eli's furnace chases away the cold and lets me breathe the tiniest bit.

"Why are you so warm, pet?" Kristoff asks. "You should be cold as ice with as much blood as I've taken."

I want to answer him, but I feel like I'm drunk. It's hard to focus, and my vision is blurry.

"Hold on, Hilda. You can beat this, beat him."

I don't know if that's true anymore.

"I swear you can, Mattie. Please hold on."

I can try to do that, but…

Blackness swallows me.

Ezekiel Crane

New Orleans, LA

I can't bring myself to move from her room. It smells like her. I've got her favorite throw in my hands as I watch over Dan. Sabien put him into some kind of dreamless sleep. As much as I want him awake to know that my little girl is okay, I know she wouldn't want him to suffer either. She loves the boy more than her own life. And I'm grateful to say Daniel loves her more than anyone, including himself and everyone around him. The connection the two of them have is scary. I've never seen anything like it. It goes deeper than the bond the Angel forged between them. It was there before he almost died. At least according to Mary.

I'm numb. I've forced myself to go numb or I'd be a mess. Memories of coming home and finding her gone when she was a baby keep haunting me. The rage from then simmers just under the surface, and all I want to do is smash things and scream. How could she do this? She knew what was waiting for her.

Ma petite is a kind and gentle soul, despite everything she's been through. It's for that reason she left. She wanted to protect Mary and her mother. Where she got her sense of right and wrong is something that baffles me. That and her morale code of ethics. I know, deep down, she's more like me than she wants to admit. She'll do what it takes to keep her loved ones safe, but she still has that niggling little voice telling her to be a good girl.

I hope that voice is gone right now. I hope she's doing everything in her power to survive. Even if it means she has to give in to her dark side.

A small knock at the door pulls me out of my own dark thoughts. Alesha Blackburne is standing there, a frown on her face. If it's more bad news, I don't want to hear it.

"Yes?" I ask, dreading her answer.

"I just came to check on Dan." She comes into the room and walks to the bed. Her hand moves back and forth over his face, and she mutters something.

"How is he?"

"He's okay for now. His mind is still at rest. Although I'm not sure that's helpful at the moment."

"What do you mean?"

She turns serious deep brown eyes on me. They remind me of my favorite dark chocolate. "His connection to her is unique. I think keeping him cut off is a mistake. We're going to need that connection to find her."

"We know where she is."

"I'm not so sure." Alesha goes and opens the windows, letting light flood the room. "We're assuming that's where she is, but we've found no evidence of that. No traffic cams caught her driving toward the bayou. Dan's partner combed every street cam, security cam, and even the ATM cameras looking for a sign of her. She came up with nothing."

"There are back roads to get where she needed to be."

"True, but she'd still have to drive past at least one camera. Did anyone check the cameras going in the opposite direction?"

"I assume…"

"And what do they say of those who assume things?" She quirks a brow. "Even your demon has his doubts. Why else would he be trying so hard to compose a locater spell?"

I'm not sure what to say to that. I thought Silas might be trying to bypass the wards on the island to go straight to her.

"Where else could she be?"

"That's the question of the hour. I might be wrong. She may be on the island."

"But you don't think so."

"No, I don't."

I rub a hand across my face. Gods, I'm tired.

"This isn't your fault."

My head snaps up. "I know that."

"You do, but you don't, not really. You're blaming yourself for not being able to keep her safe."

As much as I want to deny it, I can't. The truth is, despite all my best efforts, I wasn't able to keep her from walking out on her own. I couldn't keep my own child any safer now than I could when she was two.

"I blame myself for everything Alexandria went through." Alesha laughs mirthlessly. "For what she's *still* going through. I made a decision when she and Jason were little. I left to keep them safe. I made the best choice I could at the time, but neither of them understands that. They'll never forgive me for walking away, no matter my reasons. They can barely stand my presence as it is."

That explains why they called their mother by her given name instead of the typical Mom or Mama. "The decisions we make as parents don't always make sense to them. Sometimes it doesn't even make sense to us in the long run. All we can do is keep trying to be the best we can and hope they forgive us for the ones we get wrong."

"What about the things we can't control? I have a son I only just found out about. He grew up with a man who taught him to hate me."

Alesha comes over and takes my hand, squeezing it gently. A small spark of something sizzles under my skin where she's touching me. The sensation is odd, but I don't pull my hand away, which is even stranger. This woman calms me even when she's irritating me. Her arrogance is as bad as my own, and she doesn't apologize for it. I find myself fascinated, and it worries me enough to put up a wall between us. I've only ever come close to this kind of feeling once, and that was with Cass's mother.

"You do what I'm doing. You keep trying no matter how many times he pushes you away. You do everything in your power to make sure he understands you're here for him now, that you want a relationship with him, and that no matter what, even if he can't bring himself to accept you, you'll love him. You do love him, don't you?"

"With every fiber of my being. It doesn't matter that I just found out about him. He's my son, my flesh and blood, and it's killing me that he can't bring himself to look at me."

"It hurts. It'll keep hurting, and you just learn to live with it. But you keep trying, and you'll eventually prove to him that you love him more than anything else in this world. That you'll do anything you can for him. Our children are our hearts and our souls. They can hurt us, wound us to our core, but we'll take it and we'll shoulder it, and we'll keep doing what we can to do what's best for them. It's our joy and our burden as parents."

This woman seems to know every single fear I have about my children. Her own past mirrors mine in more ways than I feel comfortable with, but at the same time, it's easy for me to talk to her. It's the strangest thing. I've never felt like I could open up to anyone, and that includes my parents, but with Alesha…I don't understand it. I'm not even this open with Nancy.

But Nancy isn't reacting well to our world. At first, I held out the hope she'd understand. She seemed to be coping, but she's locked herself in her room. Mrs. Banks told me to let her be, that she needed to process everything. After witnessing Dan's display, I don't blame her for being afraid or needing to work through what she's seen.

I hope she comes around. It would devastate Emma Rose if her favorite person couldn't handle her being special.

Alesha understands our world, though. She lives in it, teeters on the edge of right and wrong almost every day. She knows what it's like to do what you must to keep your loved ones safe. She's like me. She's a monster who doesn't hide from her darkness. She embraces it.

In a lot of ways, she's a perfect match for me. More so than any woman I've ever been interested in. I could easily find myself…

No. I will not go there.

Nancy deserves better than my wandering thoughts. She loves me, and I love her.

Gently, I pull my hand away from Alesha, uncomfortable with the thoughts and feelings she's inspiring. I know she's only trying to help, so I don't want to hurt her feelings.

"Thank you. It helps to hear someone besides myself say that."

"You're very welcome. Is it okay if I run something by you?"

"Of course."

"Our discussion earlier got me to thinking. Maybe we're all going about this wrong."

"What?"

"We're focusing our efforts on trying to locate your daughter. What if we also try to locate the vampire himself? A locator spell just for him. He was smart enough to tamper with Madame's creatures, so why wouldn't he be smart enough to hide Emma from us? He might have some kind of magical shield around her."

"But wouldn't he have one around himself as well?"

"Possibly, but everyone slips up sometime. He might have forgotten that little detail."

"That's brilliant."

"There's only one small problem."

"And that would be?"

"I need something of his, some connection to him that might help me focus a spell."

Well, hell. "We don't have that."

"Not yet. I'm going to go out tonight and hunt down a few leads. There are still a few people in this town who owe me favors."

"It's too dangerous to go by yourself." The thought of her out there where the vampire could snatch her is not something I'm willing to chance. If Kristoff got his hands on someone as powerful as Alesha Blackburne, there's no telling what he'd be able to do.

I know exactly who the Blackburnes are. You can't grow up in New Orleans and be a part of the paranormal community without knowing who they are. My family and I never crossed paths with them, at least not that I'm aware of. Hopefully, they'll turn out to be an ally in the future.

She smiles the most charmingly evil smile I've ever seen cross a woman's face. And I like it. "Trust me, Ezekiel, Kristoff will never see me coming."

"Be that as it may…"

She puts a finger to my lips. "I can take care of myself."

Again, that strange spark ignites under my skin where she's touching me. I've never felt anything like it. And again, I like it. More than I should, considering my feelings for Nancy.

"Then let me escort you."

"No offense, but your name doesn't inspire goodwill in the places I'm going."

"And yours does?"

"My grandfather's, no, but mine? People trust me."

That much I agree with. I'd done some digging, and she and her brother both had an exemplary reputation among even the worst of us. It's why I allowed them in my home.

"What can I do?"

"Pray to whatever god or gods you worship that I find something." She gives me one last smile and leaves the room.

Dan stirs, and my gaze swings back to him. He's restless even in this supposed dreamless sleep. When I first met the boy, I didn't like his relationship with my daughter. She seemed to cling to him, and he was too old for her. But she trusted Daniel, and I had to live with it. To get to know her, I had to deal with the boy.

Over the years, he's proven to me how much he loves my daughter, that he'd give his own life for hers. The bond they have goes deeper than the soul meld performed on them. It only strengthened what was already there. I hope to God it'll prove useful to finding her before Kristoff kills her.

A sob catches in my throat at the thought of my beautiful little girl dead and lifeless. She's her own force of nature, and I hope to God I can find her. I can't lose my sweet pea again. I can't.

Sinking down on the floor beside Dan's bed, I bow my head and allow myself to cry. I haven't cried since she was taken, but I can't help it now. She's gone, and I'm as helpless as before.

Please, God, if you care for her at all, please keep her alive. I know there's no keeping her safe. But maybe God can at least keep her alive until we find her.

Please.

Mary

New Orleans, LA

Zeke is insistent I get ready for college to start. He sent me with Nathaniel, Eric, and Ethan to collect our books from the college bookstore earlier. I don't want to go. I don't want to go to school and pretend everything is normal. Because it's not. Nothing's normal.

I can't sleep. I find myself slipping back into what my therapist calls waking nightmares. They're memories that feel more like dreams and occur while I'm wide awake. Not just memories of Mrs.

Olsen, but memories of my time with Deleriel. I worked hard to put that behind me, but Mattie's situation is bringing all that back.

And with those memories, I find myself immersed back into the same state I was in when Mattie found me in Deleriel's locked room. I was a shadow of who I was. A battered and beaten-down echo. I don't talk with my family about my time there because I don't want to ever see that look of pity on their faces. My therapist knows about everything from the sexual abuse to the psychological terror.

Deleriel was honestly fascinated with me. He did everything he could to make me comfortable. But that fascination didn't stop him from hurting me. One minute he was kind, and the next...the next he was the monster who lived beneath the beautiful mask. I never knew from moment to moment who I was going to get when he walked into my gilded cage.

And underneath those memories were the ones of Mrs. Olsen. Which were some of the worst. What I went through with her blurred the line between outright torture and psychological torture. What I suffered physically with her was far worse than anything Deleriel ever did.

My leg twinges, and I rub it absently. I'll never walk right. Mrs. Olsen broke more bones in that one leg than most people would break in a lifetime. Zeke had the best specialists in the country look at it. They did help a bit, so my limp is not as bad as it was, but it's how I am now. That and the scars.

I have a multitude of scars that cover my body from the wounds Mrs. Olsen inflicted. She loved knives. I remember once she traced my entire body with a blade. She knew how deep she could push the blade and how many small cuts she could inflict without it killing me.

I'm not the same girl physically or emotionally that I was before the day she took me. I'll never be that girl again.

My phone buzzes, and I look to see a text from Nathaniel. He's taken it upon himself to make sure I'm safe. Smiling, I shake my head and text him back to say

I'm reading and to leave me alone. I don't need a watchdog. The truth is I'm glad he's paying attention. Kristoff almost had my mom. Mattie left to keep her safe, for which I will be forever grateful. I love my sister, but I love my mom too. I don't know what I'd do if she died.

Nathaniel irritates me in a way no one else ever has. I don't know from one minute to the next if I want to strangle him or…no. I will not go there. Nathaniel Buchard is evil. Yes, he loves his sister. Yes, I can see he's changing every single day. But he was raised without a conscience, and I won't put myself back into a situation with someone like that. His lack of compassion reminds me so much of Deleriel.

And I still think about what it would be like to kiss him.

And that scares the hell out of me.

The incessant ringing of the doorbell stops those thoughts in their tracks. Thank God for distractions. Getting up, I go to answer it. Mrs. Banks and Jameson are out for the afternoon. I'm not sure why, but hey. Everyone needs to get out of lockdown every once in a while.

The gorgeous aqua eyes staring at me from the other side are not what I was expecting. Benny Malone and Brandon Richards are standing on the front porch with the entire Malone and Richards clan behind them. I'd forgotten Zeke insisted they come here after what happened with Mom. I bet Mrs. B went to the grocery store.

"Hi, Mary." Benny's tone is solemn. "Did you find Mattie yet?"

"No, honey, we haven't." I step aside and open the door. "You guys come on in."

"Where's Uncle Dan?" Brandon asks. He has the same dark brown hair that Dan does, but he has his mama's blue eyes. He and Benny are the same age, so they've become good friends. Declaring themselves brothers, according to Dan.

"He's asleep right now."

"Well, wake him up," Brandon says as he drops his duffle bag to the floor. "We're here."

"I can't wake him up, Bran. We had to

put him into a magical sleep so he wouldn't be in pain."

"Pain?" James Malone's eyes narrow as he and his wife, Heather, come in. "What did those Cranes do to him?"

My irritation flares. "Absolutely nothing. He's in a magical sleep to protect him from the pain."

"Don't bother, Mary." Zeke sweeps into the room. "Please come in, and welcome to my home. I'll show you upstairs to Daniel's room in a few minutes."

"I want to see my son now." James doesn't look like he's going to take no for an answer.

"Sorry about this," Caleb whispers next to my ear, and a full body shiver goes through me. He always had the sexiest voice I've ever heard. "Dad's been like this since he found out about Mattie. He's worried about Dan and Mattie both."

James and Heather love Mattie. I know this, but I also know deep down, there has to be some resentment because she cost them Eli, and now that her life is linked to Dan's, she might cost them him too. I get it, but taking it out on Zeke isn't going to fly.

"Yes, I'm going to bother." I push out of the mass of bodies to step in front of Zeke. "Zeke has done every single thing he can to protect Dan. Not only because Mattie loves him, but because Zeke loves him too. He considers Dan one of his kids, the same as me. He invited you all into his home to keep you safe. He did that because of Dan. He knows how much you mean to him, and I'm not going to stand here and let you talk down to him. You should be *thanking* him."

James blinks several times. "You're starting to sound like a Crane, Mary."

"That's because I *am* a Crane, Mr. Malone. I may not biologically belong to Zeke, but I'm as much his daughter as Mattie is. He loves me. He's never once shown a difference between me, Mattie, Eric, and now Ethan. I'd have let him adopt me if I thought it wouldn't upset my mama."

"That you are." Zeke hugs me to his side. "You're as much my child as Emma is. Now, what say you and I get everyone settled in downstairs? Jameson, the boys, and I worked all morning to turn some of the basement rooms into makeshift bedrooms."

"I think you're going to need to build an addition to the house, one just for extra bedrooms. With The Hathaway Foundation, I think this is going to become a regular occurrence."

Ava waves at me when she comes through the door, not having heard my angry rant. "Hey, Mary! Dad says I'm bunking with you. Hope you don't mind my makeup bag." She pats the bag slung over her shoulder. It looks more like one of Silas's paint containers than a makeup bag. She's the spitting image of her mother—tall, blonde, and beautiful. The only thing she inherited from her father was his brown eyes.

Something brushes my leg, and I jump, startled.

"Sorry, that's Damien." Benny pats his leg, and I feel the massive frame go by me again. I'd forgotten Silas gave Benny his own Hellhound after the kid had been kidnapped.

Hellhound…wait…ughhhhh.

Why didn't I think of this before?

"Peaches!"

"She's at Silas's." Zeke frowns.

"No, Peaches might be able to find Mattie. Remember when Silas locked her in her room in his house, and Peaches opened a doorway back here for her? Do you think she could open one to her?"

"I don't know." Hope springs to life in Zeke's eyes, but Benny squashes it in the next breath.

"She can't. She can only go someplace she knows or to a place she can see in Mattie's head."

"But don't they hunt down people too? Can't she do that for Mattie?"

"No." Benny shakes his head. "They're collecting souls that are owed. The only way they know to do that is to kill the person and bring their soul back to their owner."

"But…"

"I already asked Silas."

"You did?" his mother asks, shocked. "When?"

"He came to check on us the night Mattie went missing. I asked him if Peaches or Damien could find her. He explained that Hellhounds are not police search and rescue dogs. They only know how to protect or to kill. There is no gray area for them."

He sounds so much older than he is. I guess after everything he's been through, he's been forced to grow up. I know I won't ever be the same; I just hate that he's like that too now.

"Maybe Alesha or her brother might be able to find a work-around on that," Zeke says softly, refusing to give up on the one thing that might get us to Mattie. I don't blame him. I'm not ready to give up on the idea yet either.

"Zeke, why don't you show everyone downstairs, and I'll take Mr. Malone up to see Dan and show Ava our room?" It's probably best to separate the two of them right now. Tempers are flaring, and neither of them needs to get into a fight. It won't solve anything.

"Of course." Zeke nods, but I can tell his mind is elsewhere. He's probably already plotting how to find a way around a Hellhound's primary initiatives. Silas breeds Hellhounds, though. He'd know better than anyone what they're capable of. I don't point that out.

I can feel Caleb's eyes on me as I head toward the stairs. I'm not ready to deal with him just yet. He and I had a long conversation the last time he was here, and while we didn't come to any kind of resolution, we ended better than when he'd arrived. I wasn't pissed off at him anymore. I get that he stayed in North Carolina to be with his family after Eli died, but he never even called, texted, or emailed me. It was like he'd cut me out of his life, and that hurt more than anything. I thought there was something there, and he swears there is, but I don't know. I don't trust him anymore.

"Here you go." I open my bedroom door and let Ava inside. "It's a king bed, so we shouldn't have any issues sharing it."

"I'm a cover hog," she warns.

"Who's a cover hog?"

I turn to see Jason Reed walking down

the hall. His girlfriend decided to walk out on us, and according to Ethan, they broke up when she did that. I'm not sure where Ethan gets his information, but he's never wrong. Seems Jason liked Bree a lot, and losing her hurt. I can see that hurt shining out of his eyes.

"Me." Ava sticks her head around the doorframe and waves. "I'm Ava Malone."

Jason stops mid-step, and his nostrils flare so wide, it's almost comical. Only this isn't funny. His eyes sharpen, deepen, and the strangest color flickers through the blue depths. I'm not sure what it is, but it's prominent.

"This is Jason Reed," I introduce them. "This is James Malone, Ava and Dan's father."

Jason's eyes haven't left Ava, and her father notices. He steps in front of her, and Jason growls. I mean a full-on doggy growl.

"Easy."

His sister and her boyfriend are right behind him. Alex puts a hand on his shoulder, and he shakes her off.

Something is definitely going on. James doesn't like it one bit either.

"This is his sister Alex and her boyfriend Luca." My gaze swings from Jason to James, gauging how dangerous this might be.

"Time to go, Jason."

He shakes his head, his nostrils so wide it's like he's snorting drugs.

"Now, Jason." A cold wind whips down the hallway, and Jason's knees wobble. The intensity of it increases, and he falls to his knees. Alex is struggling herself. What the hell is going on?

"Can you take Ava into her room, please?" Luca asks, keeping his eyes locked on Jason. "I'll take care of this."

James rushes his daughter into the room and closes the door. I'm not offended. Whatever is going on with Jason is weird, and I understand the man's need to protect his daughter.

"What's wrong?" I ask.

"It is…how you say…" Luca frowns, searching for the right word. I adore his broken accent. It's more charming than either Cass's or Nathaniel's.

"Complicated," Alex finishes for him. "And it might get more complicated."

"I don't understand."

"She's his mate," Alex explains. "Wolves only mate with one true mate, and it's for life."

Holy crap.

"Uh…" I glance at the closed door. "Her dad is an FBI agent, so yeah, it might get really complicated really fast."

"I take him back to the room and keep him there." Luca hauls him up and starts dragging him down the hall.

"How old is she?" Alex asks, worrying her lip with her teeth.

"She's eighteen, still in high school. She graduates this year, I think."

"Okay. Let us know if you need anything. I'm going to go check on my brother."

Shaking my head at this new complication, I knock on the door and wait for James to open it. Even though it's my room, I have manners.

"What the hell was that about?" he asks as soon as he sees me.

"That's a complication. Jason is a

shifter, and…"

James's eyes widen at the implication. "No. She's still in school. I will not allow it. She's not going anywhere near a shifter."

"Uh, what are you guys talking about?" Ava pushes past James. "Who's a shifter?"

"Jason."

"The cute guy from the hallway?" Her eyes widen. "Really?"

"Yeah, but it's best you stay away from him while you're here."

"Why?"

"Because…" I close my eyes, trying to find a good way to say this. I know James would rather I keep my mouth shut, but secrets have a way of coming back to haunt you later. I don't do secrets if I can help it. "Shifters have one true mate, and you're apparently his. It's not something you have to worry about here, though. Alex will keep her brother on a leash."

"He doesn't even know me!" Ava's eyes are as big as Double Stuf Oreos.

"He doesn't have to. He can smell you, and your scent has alerted his wolf that you're his fated mate."

"Absolutely not!" James shouts.

Ava ignores him.

"That's weird and yet oddly romantic."

"No." James gets in his daughter's face. "Don't even think about it. You're still in high school."

"He's right, Ava. A mate bond never goes away. It never weakens. It'll keep until after you've graduated and gone to college. Why don't I take you guys to see Dan now?"

James opens his mouth, but Ava flounces out into the hallway. He all but runs after her. Not that I blame him. Jason Reed is a hottie. Ava is going to do her best to get him alone and find out more about this. It's what I'd do.

"He has his own room here, but we put him in Mattie's room. He seems to rest better in there." I show them down the hall and open the door. Dan's sound asleep, as I told them. "He can't hear you either. Sabien has him in a dreamless state to protect him."

"I don't know if I'd call this protecting him."

"If you'd seen him doubled over and screaming in pain, you wouldn't say that. Trust me. This is kinder right now."

"Screaming?" Ava whispers. "Then that means Mattie is screaming somewhere."

"Yes."

Both their faces blanch.

"I'll let you guys visit." Backing up, I close the door behind me. Thinking of Mattie and what she's going through…

"Honey."

I almost scream when my mom's voice stops me.

"Don't do that, Mom." I place my hand over my heart. I swear, before this week is out, I'm going to have a heart attack.

"Sorry. Can you come to my room? I want to talk to you about something."

"Sure."

We head upstairs to the third floor. Zeke put my mom in the attic. There's a bed up here, but a lot of junk too. It wasn't his first choice, but the West Virginia visitors had all the other rooms.

All the lights are on upstairs, and it's still dark. Zeke needs to either add more windows, maybe a skylight or two, or just remodel the whole thing.

"What's up, Mom?" I ask, sinking down on the bed and stretching out.

"I wanted to know how you are. Do we need to have your therapist come by for a house call?"

Of course she'd be worried about my emotions.

"No, Mom, I'm fine. I get that everyone's worried memories are going to cause me to spiral out of control, but that's not true. Am I having flashbacks? Hell, yes."

"Language," she rebukes.

"Sorry. All I'm saying is I can handle it. Promise."

"You're sure?"

I nod. I'll lie through my teeth all day to keep her from worrying. I probably should talk to my therapist, but doing so would force me farther down my dark hole. If Mom knew how I was really feeling, she'd go into Mama Bear mode. I can't handle that right now.

"And how are you handling having Caleb here?"

She knows how much I liked Caleb. I even called her and told her about his last visit.

"I'm not handling it." I flash her a soft smile. "It's easier to ignore him and my feelings right now. We need to focus on finding Mattie. I'll deal with Caleb after that."

"Mary, ignoring him is only going to make it worse, especially with Nathaniel in the picture."

"Nathaniel? What does he have to do with anything?"

Moms scoffs. "Please. I've seen how he looks at you and how you look at him when you think he's not watching."

"Nope, Mom, you're wrong. I have no feelings but distrust for him."

She laughs. My mother actually laughs at me. "Honey, you look at that boy the way I looked at your father at your age."

"We're not going there, Mom. There are things you don't know about Nathaniel, things that would send you running in the opposite direction."

"I'm sure there are, just as I'm sure at least some of the rumors about Ezekiel

Crane are true. Not all people who do bad things are really bad, Mary. You should know this, given the company you keep."

I don't want to think about Mattie's brother right now any more than I do Caleb. Both are a sore spot for me.

"Can we please drop it, Mom?"

She nods, and then her expression turns serious. "I overheard what you told Dan's father about Mr. Crane. Did you mean what you said?"

"I wasn't about to stand there and let him lay into Zeke when all he's done is try to protect us all. That wasn't fair."

"No, it wasn't." My mom moves her blonde hair off her shoulder and twists it. She normally keeps it up in a bun because she works so much. I think having it free is starting to bug her. "That's not what I want to talk about, though. I heard you say you'd let Zeke adopt you."

"I…" My mouth snapped shut. I'd never meant for her to hear that. I didn't want her to get hurt. "Mom…"

She holds up her hand. "Mr. Crane has asked me about this before."

"He did?"

"Yes. He said his last name could provide you benefits that outweighed the negativity it might cause. He loves you very much, as much as your own father did. I told him no because I thought it might upset you."

"Is that the only reason?"

A small sigh escapes her. "No. I was afraid he was trying to erase your father from your past. That he wanted you to forget who you were and where you came from."

"Zeke's not like that, Mom. He'd never ask me to forget Daddy or even suggest it."

"I'm beginning to see that. Before, he was just a man who tried to help you because of how much Mattie loved you. He wanted to make her happy. That's what I told myself, at least. Being here, though, watching you interact with the entire Crane family, I have to admit that they all love you as much as they do Mattie."

"They do. Family isn't always about blood ties, Mom. It's about the people who love you and will be there for you no matter what. I love you and Daddy, but I love them too. Zeke is like a second father to me. He's never shown a difference in his love. Neither have Lila or Josiah, for that matter. They decided we belonged to them, and that was that. I know Eric's considering changing his name to Eric Crane. Zeke asked him about it a few months ago."

"Why hasn't he?"

"His parents. He's afraid it will upset them."

"They've been through a lot. I know it's hard on him that he can't remember his life with them. It was very kind of you girls to take him in after the shooting."

Mom doesn't know who Eric really is, and I'm not going to tell her either. Eric has enough on his plate without my mom giving him curious looks.

"He's family now."

"How do you feel about changing your name to Crane? I want the truth, Mary. What you said back there was in the heat of the moment, and I thought it would be good to talk about it."

That was a loaded question with the potential to hurt my mother a great deal. Something I don't want to do. But honestly? I have thought about changing my last name. Having their last name would make me feel like I belong to them even more than I do now. I love them, and that name would just be an extension of that love.

"Mom…"

"The truth, Mary Elizabeth."

She brought out the middle name. She's serious.

"Do you remember the first time Daddy made me watch one of those old John Wayne movies? I hated it. I'd rather have been watching cartoons. It became our thing, and I still watch them every Sunday."

"Your daddy loved his westerns. He told me his father watched them with him, and his grandfather watched them with his father. It was a family tradition."

"I know. He told me. He was so proud of the fact he had me to share them with. He didn't even care I was a girl."

"He told me if we were never graced with another child, he was okay with that. It just wasn't in God's plan, and we'd be happy with our girl. And he was, Mary. He loved you more than anything in this world."

"I loved him too. He taught me about tradition and family. That's why I value what I have here with the Cranes. They love me as much as you and Daddy."

"I see it. That's why I think if you want to change your last name, I'm okay with that."

"But I'm not, Mom. What I said, it was said in the heat of the moment. I was so mad, and it just slipped out. If I changed my name, it would feel like I was betraying Daddy's memory and all the family traditions he passed down to me. Having my last name as Crane doesn't mean I'm any more or less a Crane than I am now. Being a Cross, though? I'm proud of that name and the history behind it. I'm proud of Daddy, and I'd never lessen that by dropping my last name before I'm married. I'm a Cross just as much as I'm a Crane."

"Your father would be standing up, his chest out, crowing like a peacock hearing you say that." A tear slips down her cheek, and she brushes it away. "I miss him."

"I do too, Mom. Every day."

She pulls me in for a hug. "One day it'll get easier."

"I'm still waiting on that day. Maybe when I'm old and senile, I'll forget the pain."

"I'll tell you if it goes away when I'm old and senile."

"You're never going to be senile. Grandma and Grandpa had good genes."

She laughs. "They did. I used to tease Mom that she was going to be a hundred and not look a day over sixty."

Grandma Opal had really good genes. She died at sixty-two of a heart attack, but the old woman looked forty. Lila's like that too. Neither of them actually looked their age.

Mom turns serious. "If you ever decide you want to change your name, I want you to know it won't hurt my feelings, and I don't think your dad would be angry either. We both just want you happy."

"I am happy, Mom."

She quirks a brow.

"Well, I'll be happy when we get my sister back and I can stop having nightmares for good."

"You sure you don't want me to call your therapist?"

"I'm sure. If it gets to where I can't handle it, I'll call her myself."

"Do you promsie?"

"Pinkie swear." I hold out my pinkie, and she hooks hers with mine. "I'm good, Mom."

I'm not sure she believes me, but she changes the subject. "What say we go check on the guests before something else goes wrong?"

"Mary!"

Ethan's shouting from the second floor. "Mary!"

Alarmed, I jump up and run down the stairs. He's standing in the middle of the hallway, checking every bedroom.

"What's wrong?"

"Eric's gone."

Saidie

New Orleans, LA

"We have a huge problem!" Alex bursts through my bedroom door with Luca all but dragging Jason behind him. He looks stoned out of his mind. What the hell?

Luca drops him on the bed and looks to his brother. "He no good."

"Wha' happened?" Aleric asks.

"Ava Malone is what happened," Alex grouches. "She's his mate, and she's still in high school."

"Holy shit!"

"That's what I said." Alex closes the door and sends a text message, presumably to either Connor or Micah or both. "This is not good. The girl's father is an FBI agent. He'll lock Jason up if he goes anywhere near her."

"I guess it's good Bree went home after all," I mutter.

Alex either agrees or chooses to ignore that remark. "First, we have Alesha to worry about with her mate bond, and now Jason. This is not good."

That is putting it mildly.

"What's wrong with Jason?" He's lying there like he's eaten an entire plate of weed brownies or something.

"I had to make him no go near Ava. He will be fine."

I forgot that Luca basically has control over the wolves—all animals, really. He can make them do whatever he wants. Alex hates it when he goes all Romani magic animal lord because it affects her too. Then again, I'm Aleric's human servant. He can force me to do things as well, but he's never used that against me. He's never once forced his will onto mine. For which I am grateful.

"So, how are we going to keep him from doing something stupid?"

"Send him back to West Virginia." Aleric stands from the window seat and comes over by the bed. "De boy needs to be far away for de bond to stop messin' wit' him."

There's a knock at the door. Alex lets Micah and Conner in. Micah takes one look at Jason and understands what's going on. "Who?"

"The daughter of an FBI agent," Alex tells him. "Aleric thinks we should send Jason home."

"No." Conner's eyes are blown. "He needs to be here."

"Why?"

"Because she'll die if he doesn't stay. His bond with her will keep the girl safe. Something's coming, something bad. Something that has nothing to do with the island."

"What?" Alex lays her hand on his shoulder. It helps him to focus. "What do you see?"

"Something dark. I can't see its face or

even tell what kind of thing it is, but it's deadly. It's coming. If Jason's not here, I see that girl ripped to shreds, lying in a pool of blood in the hallway. That's all I see."

"Okay. Then we need to let Alesha know, and we'll take shifts with Jason. He can't be allowed near her. He doesn't have the self-control our mother does. His magic just woke up, and it's going to drive his senses into hyperawareness." Alex clenches her fists, and Luca is there in a heartbeat. "I can't let anything happen to him."

"Nothing will, *munya*. We keep him safe. Promise."

Without a word, Micah comes and wraps his arms around her from behind, his chin resting on the top of her head. "Luca's right. We're all here. Nothing is going to happen to your brother."

The three of them have some kind of weird bond I don't understand. If it were anyone else holding Alex like that, Luca would tear them apart. But not Micah. One day, I'm going to ask Alex to explain that to me.

"Why doan you t'ree go and inform de witch of dis new complication, and Saidie and I will watch over Jason."

"What about me?" Conner asks Aleric.

"I doan know. Go eat or som'tin?"

Conner laughs and rubs his belly. "I can eat."

Before we can implement our plans, Alesha opens the door. She never knocks. It's a bad habit of hers. It's why I've learned to lock my door when I want some privacy.

"The spell is ready. We should leave for the island immedi—" She breaks off when she sees all of us in the room, and then her gaze lands on Jason. "What happened?"

"His mate is what happened," Alex tells her. "She's still in high school."

"Well, damn." Without a word, she walks over to her son and whispers a single word. His eyes close, and his breathing evens out. "We don't have time to deal with this. We need to get to the island. The girl has been with that vampire longer than I'd hoped."

"She might already be dead." I don't

want to point this out, but I feel like I have to.

"She's not dead yet, because her fiancé is still breathing. According to her father, if she dies, he dies."

"Well, that's good news, in a weird way."

"Come along, children. We have a lot to do. It's going to be just us. One of the boys has disappeared, and Ezekiel and the others are searching for him. We can't wait. This needs to be done before it gets any darker."

The ride back to Madame's is grim. This is something I knew we had to do, but it's also something I don't want to do. I'm curled up in Aleric's lap, while Alex is smashed between Luca and Micah. Conner's eyes are blown wide, which means his Sight, as he calls it with a capital S, is running on steroids. I hope he sees us winning.

Aleric is stiff as a board beneath me.

"Alesha's potion is going to give us the advantage," I whisper. "Those things won't hurt us."

"That's not necessarily true," Alesha

says from the driver's seat.

"What?" I ask, alarmed. "I thought this potion was supposed to make sure I could control them."

"It does," she agrees, "but in order for you to control them, they have to touch you first."

"You never said no'tin about dem touchin' her." Aleric's eyes have gone darker, the green disappearing completely.

"The potion is bound with her blood. The moment she takes it, it becomes like a shield around her. Anything dead that touches her will succumb to her will."

"It is no' acceptable," Aleric bites out. "She will no' subject herself to dis."

"It's the only way." Alesha turns onto the dirt road leading to Bubba's dock. How she remembered where it was, I have no idea. "Do you want those things out there forever, able to kill anyone at will, Aleric? You know better than anyone how it feels to have to suffer their touch. Would you wish that on innocents?"

He growls, his hands tightening around

me. He would let anyone suffer if it meant keeping me safe. I know this, even if Alesha doesn't.

"She's right. We can't let them stay there. I survived them once, and I will survive them again."

"You doan have to do dis."

"Yes, I do. Kristoff and everything he's done is my responsibility. If I had dealt with him in the beginning, none of this would be happening now. I have to finish this, Aleric."

Bubba's not anywhere to be seen, but there are dozens of people waiting for us at the dock, their boats in tow.

"Wait here, children." Alesha steps out of the car, and we all ignore her order. We pile out right behind her. She looks annoyed but doesn't say anything.

"Are you Alesha Blackburne?" The tallest of the lot of them steps forward.

"Who's asking?"

"Robert Willow. My nephew called and said you had a way to get onto the island. We're your backup."

"I thought you refused to help the Cranes." Her tone is completely cold.

"This isn't about them. If we find the girl, we find the girl. We're here to make sure the island is cleared out of all the creatures the Necromancer had on it. We're here to protect the innocents who might stumble upon it, not to find a girl who handed herself on a silver platter to a monster."

"She did that to *protect* an innocent."

Robert just stares Alesha down, his expression hard. He really hates the Cranes. You can see it in his eyes.

"Let them stay," Alex says after a long moment. "We might need the help."

Alesha looks like she wants to argue, but she knows Alex is right. We're outnumbered, and they might be able to help. So with that, we load up onto the boats and make the ride out to the Island of The Dead.

The boats make the journey to the island as night falls. It's probably not the best time to do this, but if Emma Crane is there, we need to find her. And Kristoff needs to be dealt with.

Once and for all, that vampire is going down.

My nerves are getting the best of me. I don't know anything about any of these people except that they weren't willing to help find Emma because they don't like the Cranes. And that doesn't paint them in a very flattering light.

But they did come armed to the teeth. I even saw a few flame throwers being strapped on. It can't hurt, especially if

Kristoff turned some of those missing girls into vampires. I don't know if he has that ability, but I'm not asking Aleric where there are so many ears listening to our every word. These are hunters who will likely kill a vampire and ask questions later. I'm not putting Aleric in danger.

"Saidie," Alesha calls once we're within spitting distance of the shore.

"You really doan have to do dis, *Draga.*"

Leaning up, I kiss him. "Don't do anything stupid like jump in after me. Give me time to get control of them, okay?"

He growls his displeasure.

"Luca, you won't let him, will you?"

"No, you do what you must. I keep him here with me."

Conner stops me. "Things have changed."

"What do you mean?"

"I'm not sure. I just don't get the same sense of dread as I did before when it comes to Emma and this island. I don't know if that's good or bad."

"She might be dead, you mean?"

He nods.

"Great. Ezekiel Crane will skin us all alive if his daughter is dead."

"We'll keep you safe from him," Robert Willow promises.

I laugh in his face. "I've been around him long enough to understand there is no protecting us from him. If he thinks we're the reason Emma died, there won't be a place we can hide from him. He's that dangerous. You'd all do well to remember that, since none of you lifted a hand to help him. *He* won't forget that."

"No, and neither will the Families of Power. When you call, we won't come. I can promise you all that."

Alesha's words are as cold and dangerous as any I've ever heard, even from Madame. Alex's mother is one scary B.

Taking a deep breath, I walk over to the edge of the boat and grip the rope ladder that descends into the murky depths of the swamps. I'm not worried about gators or snakes here. The crawlers will have killed them all. Nothing living gets within the perimeter of the island.

"Wait, you need this." Alesha hands me a vial of glowing green liquid.

"This is nasty, isn't it?"

She nods.

Pulling the cork, I swallow it all at once and gag. Bad doesn't even begin to describe it. It's like drinking dirty dishwater combined with piss and three-month-old stinky socks.

"Damn, you trying to kill me?" I wheeze, my voice hoarse.

She smiles. "I hope not."

"That's not very reassuring, Alesha."

Her phone rings, and Sabien's photo flashes. "Wait, this could be important."

We're both thinking of her fiancé. If she dies, he dies.

"What do you mean, he's missing too?"

All eyes flash to her.

"No, he's not here with us." She pauses. "Of course we'll keep an eye out." She hangs up her phone and looks back to me. "Dan's missing now too."

"Her fiancé?"

"Yes, him and the boy she calls

brother. They're gone. The security cameras don't show them leaving the house, but they're gone."

"Then I guess we better get to this, then. The sooner we clear the perimeter, the sooner we can reach the house and find her."

Before I climb down, I push my Necromancy into the water, into the crawlers, and again, they're unresponsive.

"You're sure this potion will work?" I ask.

"Positive. Its acting agent is your blood, and that's the most powerful tool we have right now."

Okay. I can do this. Those damn things are going down.

Gripping the rope ladder, I wrap myself in my gift and descend into the water. There's no hiding my fear from those who can smell it, but there's nothing I can do to shield Aleric from this. He has to sit there while I wrestle for control against the creatures Madame used as a punishment for him for years. I hope Luca can restrain him until I'm done.

The water's warm, but it has a foul stench. I'd forgotten the smell. Or maybe I hadn't noticed it before. Death smells sweet to me, but today, all I'm smelling is the odor of the swamp. Slowly, I make my way to the dock and climb up. Still nothing from the depths of the water. So, what exactly activates them? Maybe I have to actually be on land?

Testing the theory, I walk backward so my eyes never leave the water until I hit the dirt path that leads up to the manor house. The first stirrings of life come from the water. I take a few more steps backward, and the water ripples as the crawlers wake up. I'm not sure if I'm ready for this, but I tell myself to buck the hell up and deal with it. Aleric did for years. I did for hours. I can handle a few minutes.

The first black, tarry hand reaches the top of the dock, and I shudder. The memory of that pain will forever be imprinted on my skin. Instead of running, I stand my ground and wait for it to emerge and crawl toward me. It doesn't take long. They move faster than I remember, but the black, gooey mess is exactly as I remember it.

The closer it comes, the more I start perspiring. Sweat breaks out across my forehead and drips down my face. My breathing quickens. Something in my chest tightens, and I look toward the boat. Aleric is standing at the rail, his expression fierce. He's scared for me. He's angry I'm doing this. But I have to, and he understands that too, which is part of why he's so mad.

The slimy hand wraps around my ankle, and I hold in the scream. It'll only upset Aleric worse. The thing crawls up my body, and I fall backward, letting it wrap itself around me. The pain is horrific. It's like someone doused me with acid then threw salt on the wounds. Only it's a hundred times more painful. It steals my breath, but not my thoughts. The potion Alesha made me drink must be helping me to fight through the horrendous agony.

Forcing the pain from my mind, I concentrate on my own Necromancy. It's a glowing ball of light at the very edge of my mind that branches out and wraps all around me. I focus that light into the crawler and push my will into it.

"*Stop!*"

It hesitates, and I barrel my power into it like a hurricane, and the thing stops. I am a descendant of the first Necromancer, and my blood, my power, is stronger than the spell commanding these creatures. It's time they realized that. I shove my will into it with everything I have.

It freezes, and the pain goes away. I scramble out from under it, but I see dozens more making their way toward me.

Gathering all the power I have and pulling some from Aleric, I push the same hurricane force winds into every crawler I can sense and force them to stop.

"I've got them!" I shout to Alesha and the others. "You can come ashore!"

The hunters are hesitant. These things killed a few of their own. I understand their hesitancy, but it's perfectly safe.

"They won't hurt you," I promise. "They've been deactivated."

"You sure, *chèr*?" a hunter asks me and pushes his booted toe at one of them.

"Yes, I'm sure. We need to gather them all into a pile so I can put them to rest."

"You want us to touch them?" Robert looks alarmed at the prospect.

"Yes. I have to walk a blood circle around them. I can't do several small circles, especially not dozens. Luca, can you get the last four out of the water, please?"

Luca dives into the water without hesitation. He's never felt the pain their touch causes.

"Why doan we go on up to de house and start looking…"

"No." I cut him off. "There are things in that house that will overwhelm you if I'm not there. This is why you brought me in, is it not? To deal with the dead?"

"Well, yes…"

"Then let me do my job."

"Why can't we just torch them?" Robert asks, watching Luca drag one of the things out of the water.

"Because they were brought back through death magic. If you burn them, they'll just reform their shape from the ashes. They have to be put back into the ground by the same method they were pulled from it. Can your men help gathering the bodies?"

Robert nods and signals to the men standing around to start dragging the creatures into a pile. Even Aleric picks one up and drops it on the growing mound. I think he did it more to reassure himself than to actually help, but that's fine. He's suffered more than anyone here at the hands of these creatures.

Once they are all gathered, I step up to them, and Aleric hands me a wicked-looking blade. This kind of magic requires a deeper blood sacrifice. Without looking, I slice my arm. The pain is fierce, but I ignore it as I walk a circle around the bodies, coming to a stop where I began. I rub my fingers in my blood and smear it over my cheeks, and I feel the circle snap into place around me. I squeeze more blood out of my arm and drip it over the waiting dead, who stare at me helplessly. They don't want to be here any more than I want them here. They are ready to go back into the earth.

"Blood to blood, death to death, I offer up these souls to return to the earth from which they were taken."

The force that is my death magic, my Necromancy, gathers within me and bends outward toward the waiting corpses. A moan rises from them, shifting to a wail as the spirits come to collect them.

One more sacrifice to send them home.

I slice the inside of my other arm and walk the circle again, offering my blood once more to appease the spirits. When I stop and let the last drop fall, a gust of wind rushes through me, and I fall, landing on my back. I watch as the essence that animated the crawlers seeps out of their bodies and lifts skyward. I sit up in time to see the corpses begin to disintegrate back into the soil beneath them until they're all gone. They've been returned to their rightful sleep.

It drained me more than I care to

admit, but I feel Aleric's strength soaking into my bones, refueling me.

As soon as I turn to face the group, Aleric rushes to me and pulls me tight. "Are you okay, *bon fille*?"

I nod, not trusting my voice.

"How did you do that?" Robert asks, coming over to where we are. "I've never seen anything like it."

"I'm a Necromancer. It's what I do. I can no more explain it than you can go without breathing." My voice is shaky, which is why I didn't want to talk, but I have to keep the hunters from thinking I'm something to be hunted.

Robert looks like he has more questions, but Alesha intervenes. "What do we have to look forward to as we make our way inside?"

"Dey be dead roaming de island, but dey ain't like dese. I'm no' sure if dey can be killed wit'out a Necromancer's intervention. Inside, you worry about de basement. Dey be t'ings dere dat not even Madame let out wit'out taking precautions."

Robert's gaze lands on Aleric. "How

do you know so much about the island?"

"Because I was a slave here until I escaped wit' Saidie. Madame took me from my home when I was but a boy."

"Let's sweep the grounds before we go inside." Micah looks around. "I'm a shifter, and as you know, shifters retain their minds, so when I shift, don't shoot me."

"The first person who shoots him be the first to die." Luca's voice is like hell freezing over. He looks scarier than anything I've ever faced.

"No one will shoot him. We let shifters tend to their own." Another man steps forward. "I'm Christian Laroaunt. I give you my word you'll be safe."

"Conner?" Alex calls, reminding me they're both here. They'd been so quiet I forgot.

"Yeah?"

"What do you see?"

"I don't see the carnage I saw before. I see danger, but I don't think it's anything we can't handle."

"You see visions, boy?" Robert asks.

"Yes, sir. I have the Sight, thanks to

my grandmother."

"We have a Seer in our community, but he was too far away to get here in time. It's good to have you among us."

Conner doesn't say anything. His eyes have gone glassy again.

"He's watching his shifting visions. Don't be offended if he doesn't say much." Alex lays a hand on his arm. "He'll warn us if there's something we need to know."

The sound of crunching bones brings my attention back to Micah. Watching a shifter reform into his animal half reminds us all to be glad we're not shifters. Shifting hurts. Maybe not as much as the crawlers, but enough that I never want to find out how it really feels. Alex has told me enough stories.

"I think we're ready. Let's leave a guard here to make sure no unexpected surprises come our way. You can see the back of the manor from this vantagepoint. If something comes out the door, we'll know about it." Robert nods to one of the younger hunters who looks a little like him. His son, maybe?

Alesha agrees, and we spread out, our hunting mission beginning in earnest.

We stay within three feet of each other as we fan out and start walking toward the woods surrounding the property. It's bringing back bad memories for me. The last time I was in these woods, I was being chased by a possessed Aleric and trying to fight off zombies. I hate this place so damn much.

Darkness is falling, the twilight fading into true night. We should have done this in the daylight, but we're running out of time. The things on this island respond to blood magic, magic born out of the blackness of the night. They thrive when the light fades.

A shuffling comes from the left, and I

turn to see a shambling zombie, only it's not shambling as much as outright running toward us. I forgot how fast these things are. They're definitely not the zombies of *The Walking Dead*. These things can move like lightning.

A sword whistles through the air and cuts its head off. The body goes down, but I'm not sure where the head landed. The body twitches and then rises. I figured this was going to happen.

Stepping forward, I sweep my magic outward, feeling for the death on the island, for the dead roaming the outside. It's weird that I can pinpoint each one. It's like small dots on a map only I can see.

"Stand back."

The hunters move behind me as I gather each zombie to me, pulling them all to stand in one spot. This is more than dozens. This is hundreds. I don't have enough blood in my body to send them all to their graves.

"Can you torch them and see what happens?" I ask, trying to figure out how I can put them to rest.

"We sure can." Christian steps forward and pulls out his flamethrower and uses it on the zombies massed in the huddle. More are coming, but if the flames don't work for this bunch, we'll need to figure something out.

He sets fire to the first lot I have gathered, maybe forty or fifty of them. Its eerie the way they stand there, burning, waiting for my command. It's painful to watch. I actually feel sorry for them. Whatever Madame did to them surpassed her death…no. Her power became mine. They didn't die because I'm still alive, which is worse. This is my fault. I let years go by. I let them suffer for years because I was too afraid to face what I should have.

"This isn't working." Christian shuts off the flame thrower. Their bodies are reforming from the ash, just as I'd suspected. "Now what?"

"Alesha, is there anything you can do?" I look around as more and more of them come toward us. "I can't put them all down without blood, and I'm not bleeding out."

"Yes. Can you gather them here and leave them? I'll text Sabien, and he'll bring what we need."

"Tell him to stop in my room and open the closet. There are three jars on the top shelf I'll need since I'm not using my own blood."

She nods and pulls out her phone while I wrangle the rest of the pack and give them instructions to wait here until I return. It's so much easier than it was the first time I tried this. Alesha found me a really good tutor. She wasn't a real Necromancer, but she did use blood magic and was able to help me learn to use it as well. Without trying to murder me, I might add.

"Is there anything else out here we need to worry about?" I ask Aleric.

"I'm no' sure. She never tol' us all her secrets. And Kristoff might have put more measures in place. I just doan know, *ma fille*."

"Then let's work on the assumption we have it clear and head to the house."

Decision made, we trek back through the woods and make our way to the back entrance of the manor. The door is not locked, but why would Kristoff lock it? He had all those monsters guarding him. And the lights work, thankfully. It would have been a hell of a hard job trying to do this in the dark.

"Let's us clear each floor before we tackle the basement," Robert suggests. "It's what we're here for."

"That will work. Keep an eye out for the girl." Alesha's expression is fierce. She's letting them know what will happen if they find Emma and something accidentally happens to her. These guys do not like her, and if we weren't here, I think they might try to hurt her.

"Of course." Robert and his team tackle the main floor while Christian's team heads up the back stairs. Neither of them asked for Aleric's help. I don't think they trust him very much. He and his brother just give off that vibe.

Micah pads through the kitchen, his nose twitching. Alex leans down and strokes his fur to calm him. He has to smell everything in this house, and I don't envy him.

"Do you trust them to actually tell us if they find her?" Alex asks after a minute.

"No, not really."

She turns back to the wolf, and he takes off.

"*Our* backup," she explains.

"Smart."

Aleric wraps his arms around me. "Are you good, *Draga*?"

"No, but we have to do this. Not just for Emma, but for everyone."

"Aleric, do you know how many creatures are in the basement rooms?" Alesha asks as she approaches the door.

A wail comes from upstairs, and I hear the flame thrower flare up.

"Can Kristoff create vampires?" I whisper.

"No. It was why she had Lucien do all her turns."

"Maybe he collected some strays, then, because I'm feeling at least four more of them in this house."

Alesha backs us all away from the doorway and faces it like a warrior princess, her stance that of a fighter. Whatever she's muttering, I don't think it bodes well for any vampire that enters the kitchen.

"Basement," I remind him.

"When I was here last, dey were t'ree. She kept de doors locked wit' magic, warning us de creatures could kill us if we got near dem."

"Three," Alex mutters. "Maybe not so bad, then."

"Dey be bad. Doan t'ink dey woan be hard to take down," Aleric warns. "All dose creatures were bred for was to kill."

A howl echoes through the house, and then more screaming ensues from upstairs. Seems Micah joined the fight. Alex tenses, and Luca does his best to calm her. I don't know how well shifters can defend against vampires. They're really fast.

"He'll be fine," Alesha assures her daughter. "Shifters are the natural enemy of vampires. We're built to fight them."

Alex doesn't look reassured, but I guess neither would I. It's easy to say shifters are built to fight vampires when you're not the one doing the fighting.

"Come sit. You need to rest." Aleric

pulls out a chair and guides me to it. I do need to rest. I feel wiped out despite the strength I can pull from Aleric. I'm not pulling as much from him as I could, though. He needs to be on his game for whatever's downstairs in the basement.

Alesha's in front of the basement door doing whatever she's doing. I think she's checking for magical wards guarding whatever's down there. It wouldn't do to open the door and get blasted from a spell packing the same punch as a shotgun to the face.

"There's something there." Alex goes to stand next to her mother and holds out her hand.

"I don't sense anything."

"I do." She presses her hand to the door and gasps, jerking back like she's been burned. It's only when she turns that I see her hand is blistered.

"Let me see that." Alesha takes Alex's hand. "This is nasty. It's going to need to be seen to. Luca, can you take her back to the boat? We can handle what's here."

"No. I'm here in case you need some more juice." I can see the tears in her eyes, but she's fighting through the pain. "You didn't even sense the spell on that door. You need me."

"You might be right, but you're still my daughter, and your safety will always come first with me. Luca, carry her out of here if she doesn't go willingly."

Luca doesn't even wait. He just picks her up and walks out of the house. I hear her shouting as she goes. I'm not sure sending her away was the right decision, but her hand looked hella bad. I'm thinking she has second degree burns, at the very least.

Alesha turns back to the door and starts her mumbling again while the rest of us wait.

An hour passes before hunters troop back into the kitchen looking a little more harried than before. Several are bleeding, and all of them are speckled with bruises. Micah trots in, his fur splattered with blood. Conner opens the back door, and he trots out. His priority right now is Alex.

"No sign of the girl?" Alesha asks as she runs her fingertips over every inch of the door.

"No. There were more than a few vampires, but no sign of the Crane girl." Christian turns the water on in the sink and washes the blood off him. The other hunters line up to do the same. "If she's here, she's in the basement."

"She's not here." Conner lays his hands on the wall beside the door. "All I sense down there is darkness. No signs of life."

"This is what I was afraid of," Alesha mutters. "This served as a distraction. Kristoff could have her hoarded away anywhere."

"So, the vampire's not here either, then." Christian looks disgruntled.

"Probably not," I tell him. "Kristoff is a lot of things, but stupid is not one of them."

"You know him well?"

"I wouldn't say well. The little interaction I had with him while I was here was enough to make me terrified of him. You could see the madness in his eyes. He loved to hurt people, and the day Aleric helped me escape, Madame had told me she was going to let Kristoff play with me."

"Why were you here?"

"My Necromancy had just woken up, and Madame was to be my tutor. That was the plan until she decided to murder me for my gifts, anyway."

"And you," Robert turns his attention to Aleric, "you helped her? Why?"

"I suffered at Madame's hands. I'd been given to Kristoff as a punishment more den a few times. I know wha' he likes to do. I couldn't let dat happen to Saidie. She didn't deserve dat. I waited until de vampires were sleeping, and we escaped t'rough de swamp."

"Why didn't you do that before?" Robert presses.

"Because I had been a prisoner of Madame's since I was but a small boy. You get used to wha' you know, and she was all I knew."

"Leave it alone, Robert," Christian warns. "He's been through enough."

From his tone, I have to wonder if Christian hadn't suffered at the hands of someone who was supposed to take care of him.

Robert nods. "Ready to go downstairs?"

"Almost," Alesha murmurs. "I need you all to stand out of direct sight of the door. It's already injured my daughter. I don't want any more casualties."

Everyone, including Alesha, moves to the side of the kitchen. She closes her eyes and holds out her hand. The door springs open, and with it, a magical ball of fire flies out from the darkness, catching the curtains of the back door on fire.

One of the hunters closest to the back door rushes to try to put it out as Alesha yells, *"No!"* The fire jumps from the curtain to the hunter.

He screams as the flames cover him from head to toe.

"Don't touch him!" Alesha runs over and holds out her hands. A bubble forms in her hands, and with another whispered spell, the fire is drawn into the bubble where it sits, angry and jumping at the walls of its prison.

"We need wet sheets," Christian says

and sends several of the hunters upstairs. "What the hell was that?"

"A fire demon," Alesha says. "It's a lower level demon, one that is almost undetectable. Had Alex not felt it and placed her hand on the door, I wouldn't have known it was there. Its sole purpose is to cause mayhem and to harm as many living things as it can. I have it contained until I can find a way to send it home." She sets the flame on the kitchen table. "I would advise you all not to touch this."

"Not a problem," Christian says. "Is it safe to go down the stairs now?"

"I honestly don't know."

The other hunters return with the sheets, and Christian wets them and places them over their wounded comrade. He instructs two more to carry the poor man back to the boat.

"I guess we're ready now." Christian turns a grim face toward the basement. "Or as ready as we'll ever be."

With that, he descends into the darkness.

All the hunters go first. I'm not sure that's a good idea given what just happened with the fire demon, but Alesha doesn't look as worried. Conner pulls up the rear. I'd rather have him upstairs, but as he pointed out, how would he tell us if something comes up that we need to know about?

Then again, his visions aren't as strong without Alex nearby. She's a catalyst for all our unique gifts. Mine and Conner's didn't wake up until we met her. I blamed her for a long time, but she's my best friend. I can't hate her forever. I missed her too much.

Aleric stops on the steps right in front

of me, and I plow into his back. Dammit. What is he doing?

"Aleric."

"Shhh," he whispers, and the hairs on my arms stand up. Something's at the bottom of the stairs.

There's a scuffle below, and I hear the hunters cursing.

"What is it?"

"I doan know."

Instead of asking more questions, I push my Necromancy out ahead of us. What's at the bottom of the stairs is not dead, though. I get a sense of darkness, but not death. It's your average, ordinary monster. I push deeper into the basement, and the rush of death that greets me almost knocks me down. These things are hungry. Starving. It feels like they haven't been fed since Madame died.

And maybe they haven't. Perhaps Madame set up a lock and Kristoff never attempted to open it. Or maybe it was Kristoff who put the demon lock in place. It doesn't matter, really. The end result is the same. These monsters have been ignored and neglected for almost two years.

"It's safe," Robert calls, and Aleric cautiously descends, making the rest of us go slower than necessary. There's a mutilated mess at the bottom of the stairs. Black, gooey blood is splattered everywhere.

"What is that thing?" I ask.

"Something we've never seen before." Christian shakes his head. "It looks more like a Frankenstein monster than anything else."

"Madame experimented on t'ings." Aleric's voice is hushed in the quiet of the basement. A cold sweat has broken out over his forehead. His hand is not quite steady when he shoves it through his hair.

Robert is watching him closely. Vampires don't sweat. Their hearts don't beat. They don't eat. Aleric defies all those things. It's his beating heart. While he doesn't age, other bodily functions have returned to him, including the working of his digestive system. It's unique, and even Alesha and Sabien are shocked by it. They know of no other vampire who mimics everything Aleric can do since my blood restarted his heart.

Hopefully, what he sees will put Robert's thoughts to rest. Aleric is acting more like a living, breathing person than a heartless vampire.

"I need to go first from here on out." I attempt to push past my overprotective boyfriend, but he's like a solid block of stone—unmovable.

"No, you doan." He pushes me behind him. "Dey be dangerous t'ings down here."

"I know that. I can feel them. None of you can deal with the dead. It's why I'm here, Aleric. I need to do this."

His lips purse.

"Son, I know your first instinct is to shield her, to protect her from every danger you sense, but she's a Necromancer. She's the only one of us who can even attempt to stop the things down here." Robert lays a hand on his shoulder, and Aleric stiffens. He hates people touching him. At least he's not cold. Since his heart restarted, he has the normal temperature of the living. "Let your woman do what she needs to."

Aleric doesn't look too happy, but he allows me to slide out from behind him. I love that he wants to protect me, but Robert's right. He can't protect me from the dead. He'll never be able to keep me from having to deal with them.

Several bright flashlights flood the hallway. I have to ask them where they got something that bright. It would be a good tool to have in my arsenal.

There are twelve doors, six on each side of the hallway, spaced evenly apart. All but three stand open. Taking a deep breath, I approach the first closed door. It's only a few feet from me. As soon as the dead sense me, the door begins to shudder as it tries to break through. Madame must have fed them from her own blood, or they wouldn't be this crazed. Normal animal blood would keep them content, but this thing is no more normal than I am.

I push my power into it, and its mad escape effort stops. It's almost docile as it feeds from the energy I'm giving it.

"This isn't going to work," I say after a

minute.

"What do you mean?"

"It's feeding from my energy. I'm only making it stronger. Madame created it with her own Necromancy, and she fed it from herself. It gets stronger with every ounce of magic I try to push into it."

"Then how are we going to stop it?"

A bright light appears in the center of the hallway, and a woman is standing there in the afterglow. She's wearing a sundress, and her long blonde hair is done up in some kind of intricate braid. She looks around curiously.

"Who is the Necromancer?" Her voice is just as beautiful as she is.

"Who are you?" Robert bites out, his shotgun held at the ready.

"I'm someone here to help. Ezekiel sent me."

"I'm the Necromancer." I step forward, unafraid of this woman. She seems kind.

Her smile is like the warmth of a blanket on a cold winter's day. "Hello, child. What is your name?"

"Saidie."

"Saidie." She nods. "These things are

not something you can handle. They have been warped and twisted into things that no one should ever lay eyes upon. I am here to take them someplace where they cannot hurt anyone ever again."

"We have to kill them," Robert says. "They're too dangerous."

"What was done to them was through no fault of their own. They did not ask to be pulled from their graves and mutated into monsters."

"Can they be killed?" Christian asks.

"Of course they can. All creatures that are made can be unmade. None of you possess the ability to kill these things, though. Opening their doors will only result in your own deaths."

"But you can do what we can't?"

"I can." She nods.

"Who are you?"

"I am Rhea, and that is all you need to know."

"Why haven't you come before now if you've had the ability to clear the house?" I ask, unsure if I should trust her or not.

"I had no reason to be concerned with

this place before today. Ezekiel and Cass called upon me. They requested I come and help. It is the only reason I stopped searching for Rose."

"Rose...do you mean Emma Rose, Ezekiel's daughter?"

"Yes. She is my first priority. I knew she was not here, though."

"You did?"

"I came here first and moved on when I saw she wasn't here."

"And you didn't do anything to stop the things on the island?" Robert asks, aghast.

"Why would I? They did not concern me."

Her words are matter-of-fact. Whoever this woman is, kind or not, I'm not sure she has a conscience.

Before I can say anything, she glides through the first door. We see a burst of light beneath the door, and then she opens the door. She repeats this for the next two doors she comes to until all the doors are standing open.

"There, they are all taken care of."

"Are there any other creatures on the

island we don't know about?"

"Of course. This island is full of horrors."

"Could you clean the island for us before you move on? I don't know Emma well, but she seems to be someone who would never leave dangerous things unattended for innocents to walk into." Alesha grips her hands tightly.

Rhea cocks her head and walks forward. She leans in and sniffs Alesha. Her entire expression morphs into one of anger. "He doesn't belong to you."

"I...what?"

"He belongs to me." Her honey-colored eyes have darkened to pools of gold.

"He doesn't belong to either of us," Alesha says sadly. "He belongs to someone else."

"Your claim on him is stronger than hers." Rhea leans back on her heels. "Your claim to him is more dangerous than hers."

"My claim means nothing if he doesn't choose it, and that's not what matters right now. Finding Emma is our main priority once this island is cleansed."

Rhea studies Alesha, and I feel the need to speak up. "I agree with Alesha. I don't think Emma would walk away from this place until it's safe."

"No, she wouldn't," Rhea agrees at last. "I'm not sure where she gets her kindness from, given the amount of suffering she's gone through. She should be hard and cold, but she's not. She's kind and generous, helping those who don't want or deserve her help." That is directed at the hunters around us. "Fine. I shall cleanse the island so no horrors remain. I'll even heal those who are wounded before I leave. And Saidie?"

"Yeah?"

"If you ever need help, just call my name, and I will come."

And with that, she's gone. Poofed out of existence.

"Who the hell was that?"

"I doan know," Aleric whispers, "but she is someone important."

That much I know. "Come on. Let's get back to the boat and check on everyone."

Maybe she healed them, maybe she didn't. Either way, we need to get back quickly so we can get them to the ER if they're still hurt.

Emma/Mattie

Fulsome Sanitarium, MO

Ralph comes in and cringes at the waste bucket. He hates changing it as much as I hate using it, but it's all that's afforded to me. He sets a Wendy's bag down on the floor to deal with the makeshift potty.

It's getting harder and harder to get off this mattress. Kristoff has fed so much I'm not sure how much I have left in me. Which terrifies me. If Eli weren't here, I might have sunk into a depression I can't come out of.

It hurts to move. Kristoff decided I needed to suffer for making him worry, and he beat me. I'm fairly sure my ribs are broken, and I might have a broken leg to go along with my broken arm. I've gotten so used to Silas healing me that dealing with injuries for longer than an hour or two has been hard. I'm in a lot of pain, which I'm sure Kristoff loves. Constant pain drives down the will to survive.

Ralph carries the bucket out of the room. He didn't lock the door behind him. All I have to do is get up and sneak out.

"That's right, Hilda. Get up and run."

"I'm too tired," I say.

"I know, but this is your chance, Mattie. You have to try."

I'm not even sure I can get up, but Eli's right. I have to try. Dan would want me to try.

Pushing up, I whimper at the pain that assaults me from every angle. It hurts. It's not as bad as the pain I was in when I smashed my soul to kill Deleriel. It's not even as bad as my injuries after Mrs.

Olsen smashed my hands. I survived both those events, and I'll survive this. I'm Mattie Louise Hathaway. I can do this.

Using my good leg, I stand and slowly make my way to the door. Creaking it open, I look out and don't see Ralph anywhere. Wherever he's dumping my crap bucket, it must not be nearby.

The ghosts are out there, though. I feel them. It's like a cold wind that wraps around me and sinks into my bones. It hurts as much as the injuries I've sustained. Slinking to the side, I find the wall and make my way toward the stairs. I know where they are. Eli is right beside me, whispering encouragement.

But he can't stave off the feel of icy fingers clutching at me or the hot, putrid breath of the ghost who's right in my face. I can't see him, and right now that's a plus. God knows what he'd look like.

More and more of them surround me, press in on me. Fingers tangle in my hair and yank.

"Back off," I say, my voice low and rough. "I'm not afraid of you."

An eerie laugh echoes around me right

before I go flying through the air. I land on my back, the breath knocked out of me. It only takes seconds for the hands to reach for me. One grabs my ankle, and I fight to regain my breath. *They are not going to win. They will not win. They will not win.*

More laughter echoes around me, and I wonder if I said that out loud. The ghosts can hear me whether I'm speaking or not. Or at least they could before the collar.

Getting up, I fight my way down the hall, heading for the stairway. Just a few more steps.

"Mattie?"

My head jerks up. Dan? Maybe it's my mind playing tricks on me.

"Mattie, are you here?"

His voice is coming from upstairs, and I fight through the pain as I hop up each step, looking behind me to make sure Ralph hasn't followed.

"Hilda?" Eli's voice fades as I get closer and closer to the door at the top of the stairs. Maybe I don't need him now that Dan's here. He said he'd be with me for as long as I needed him.

The door creaks loudly when I crack it open and look down the narrow hallway for Ralph. Still no sign of him. Stepping out, I look to the right and to the left. Crumbling walls greet me. I remember passing this way on my first night, so I just retrace the same steps. It takes longer, and a trail of cold air surrounds me as I make my way closer to where I think Dan called from.

"Mattie?"

Again, I hear him, and I want to call out, but I'm afraid Ralph or Kristoff will hear me. I wish he'd stop calling out for the same reason. I don't know if I can protect him in the condition I'm in.

"Mattie, where are you?"

I step around a corner that empties out into what must have been the main entrance for the hospital at one time. Only broken furniture litters the floor, and the walls have disintegrated in certain areas, allowing the moonlight to shine through. It's more like the set of a horror movie than an actual place. Only it's a hundred times more terrifying because I can't see the threats. I feel them, but I can't see them. I swear I will never complain about my abilities again when I get out of this.

Dan's standing in the middle of the room, his flashlight casting around. He looks tired and drained, but just the sight of him causes hope to surge. I knew he'd find me. He's like Eli in that way. Those two could always find me no matter where I was.

"Dan?" I whisper.

His head turns toward me, and relief sweeps over his face. He rushes me and pulls me into a hug. I can't stop the scream from leaving me when he crushes my busted ribs.

"What, what is it?"

"Ribs," I wheeze.

"You're alive." He breathes the words out and hugs me tighter. "Thank you, God." He chants that over and over, hugging me again, but more careful of my injuries. "Eric and I broke out of the mansion and came here. I just had this gut feeling right in my chest. I knew I could find you."

"Eric?" I look up. "Where is he?"

"I told him to stay by the car, and if I wasn't back in ten minutes to call the cops and come looking for me."

Tears blur my vision. Of course my boys would find me. They love me more than anyone else, and that includes Zeke and Mary. I know my papa loves me more than his own life, but the bond I have with Eric and Dan transcends death. They both turned away from the light for me, and it's a debt I'll never be able to repay. I love them so much.

"Can we get out of here? Ralph is around here somewhere."

"Ralph? Who's Ralph?" His eyes scan the area much like mine do when I'm looking for the ghosts who don't want to show themselves.

"Kristoff's ghoul. He can't die, so let's get gone, please."

"Can you walk?"

"I walked this far. I can go a little farther."

A noise rattles to the left of us, and we turn our heads in unison. Nothing's there. Has to be one of the ghosts getting noisy.

"Wait here. I want to make sure the

coast is clear."

I reach for him, but he's moving away from me, toward the area we heard the noise come from. He looks around, shining his flashlight into corners. It barely cuts through the darkness since it's not one of ours from the tech vans. He should have stopped long enough to filch one.

Once he's satisfied, he starts back my way.

He makes it halfway before Ralph catches him around the neck.

"No, don't hurt him."

Ralph smiles, and before Dan can do anything, Ralph's other hand comes up, the knife in it gliding across Dan's throat. Blood wells up, and he gurgles, struggling against the ghoul's hold.

I blink, and this overwhelming sense of loss and pain claws its way through the collar, forcing feelings into my chest. I shake as I feel the life bleed out of half of my soul.

When he drops to the floor lifeless, I can't move.

I can't breathe.

His dead eyes are staring right at me, the dark, warm chocolate glassy, unseeing.

A scream rips out of my throat, and I fall to the ground, unable to function.

He's not dead.

But I feel it.

I feel his loss.

My strength drains slowly out of my limbs, and I clutch at my throat as his death tries to overtake me, tries to eat me up and claim me.

"Did you really think it would be this easy to escape?"

Ralph is standing above me, and I can't move my eyes from Dan's lifeless body, the growing pool around his head as what's left of his blood empties out onto the broken white tile of the floor.

"You killed him," I whisper.

"Yes, and now I have to move you to the second location. If he found you, others will too."

He reaches for me, and as soon as his clammy skin touches mine, this uncontrollable rage surfaces. He killed him. He killed Dan.

Anger I've only ever known when Dan's life is threatened beats at the collar. It screams to be let free, and for once, I completely give in to the darkness that lives in me. I welcome it. I need it to live. To make this right.

When Ralph is within distance, my fingers curl around his throat, and I let the last of the strength I have come forth. I will rip his head off. He might have certain protections, but even the dead need their body parts.

He struggles, but I pay him no mind as I force him down and straddle him. My fingers sink into his skin, and I pull, my only intent separating his head from his body. It takes everything I have, but it comes loose with a wet pop.

I let it fall from my hands and stagger off him.

"Bravo, pet, bravo."

Kristoff is leaning against the registration desk, clapping, his blond hair perfectly styled. He looks like he's just walked off a runway shoot for *GQ Magazine*.

"I wondered what you'd do." He

comes over and strokes my cheek. "How did it feel to kill him?"

"It felt good." I spit in Kristoff's face. "You'll need another ghoul now."

"No, he won't." Ralph comes out of the shadows.

I. Don't. Understand.

I killed him.

I did.

"It wasn't Ralph you murdered, pet."

I look toward the mess on the floor and stumble backward.

No.

No.

No.

No.

Eric is lying there, dead. His head twisted from his body.

Dan is dead a few feet from him.

I. Don't. Understand.

"I did kill Dan," Ralph explains, "but it was the boy who rushed in, hearing you scream. He got to you before I did, and Kristoff merely let you think it was me trying to pick you up. I stayed in the shadows so you wouldn't see me."

I shake my head, refusing to believe it.

I can't have killed Eric. I can't.

He's not dead.

Crawling to where he is, I try to make sense of this.

It's not Eric. It's another trick.

This is all one big trick.

"You're making me think this."

"No, pet, I'm not. You murdered the boy you called your brother, the boy who risked his own soul to keep you safe. You did that, not me."

A keening wail echoes around me, and I want whoever it is to shut up. I cover my ears with my hands, trying to shut it out. I can't unsee what's right in front of me.

"Get her. We need to leave." Kristoff gestures toward me, and Ralph nods, his feet bringing him toward me.

There is a place that lives inside me. A place I've only ever gone twice in my life. It's a place that scares me because I know I can kill in that place and never feel remorse. It's a place of solid white nothingness. A place of cold and no regret.

It's that place I retreat into, and the

keening stops. Everything stops. The pain, my anger, my grief, my guilt. It all goes away. And in its place is the girl I was born to be, the girl I ran from even when I faced Deleriel.

This is Mattie Louise Hathaway, the girl Eli told me to be.

The girl who survives.

I look up, staring him right in the eyes.

Ralph stops and takes a step back.

I know my face is calm. Neutral.

Blank.

Empty.

Scary.

I know what to do. I've always known, but deep down I was afraid to do it because I don't know if I can come back from this. I was waiting for someone to rescue me, but in reality, I don't need anyone to rescue me but myself.

"Peaches."

I know she'll hear me. She always hears me. My Hellhound will always come when I call her.

"Your dog can't find you here. That collar prevents it." Kristoff is smirking.

I smile, and it's full of teeth. "You

don't know the first thing about Hellhounds, Kristoff. You may know she's mine, but you didn't delve deeper than that."

Scratching comes from outside, and a howl reaches us. It's terrifying because it's the sound of Hell coming for you. Ralph and Kristoff look alarmed.

"I told you."

The doorframe cracks under her weight, and the door splinters, bursting inward. She comes straight for me, and I bury my head in her fur. She's in full Hellhound mode, which means she's three times my size, but it doesn't matter. I take comfort in her. Hellhounds have always calmed me. Perhaps because of my demon blood. Doesn't matter, really. All that matters is the people in front of me are going to die—and die screaming.

I lean back. "Get this off me, girl." I tug at the collar on my neck, and the hound leans down to sniff it. She growls, and the force of it almost knocks me down, but I use a handful of her midnight fur to steady myself.

Her tongue washes at my neck, and I

feel the collar expand, tightening around my neck. Her teeth sink into it and me, but she pulls it off. Blood drips down my throat from the wounds, but I'm free.

All that darkness swarms me once again as soon as I see Dan and Eric lying on the floor. Rage unlike anything I've ever known swells up and bleeds into the cold, quiet place.

My hand flexes, and I pull what I need out of my bag of tricks. My fingers form into massive claws, and I snarl, launching myself at Ralph. He tries to run, but I'm faster.

Oh, no, you don't.

I bring him down, and my knees land in his back. I see Kristoff disappear out the front door. I'll deal with him later. Right now, this thing is dying.

First, I pull his right hand back and yank his index finger off. One by one, I remove his fingers. Then I turn to his other hand and repeat the process. I rip his hands off after that. Next come his toes and then his feet. Through it all, his screams surround us, and I smile, relishing how it feels to hurt this thing, this monster.

I rip and tear until every single piece of him in lying in shreds around us. My hands become glowing balls of fire, and I unleash it onto the parts, until nothing but ash remains. He will not be coming back.

"Peaches, bring me Kristoff. Do *not* kill him. I have plans for him."

My gaze sweeps back to the boys. The calm has returned. My rage dissipated with the carnage I wrought on Ralph.

I feel nothing. I'm dead inside, which is exactly how I was born. I am Death, and everyone is going to understand that very soon.

I'll come back for the bodies later.

I have things to do first.

Cass

New Orleans, LA

Dis is no' good. Both Eric and Dan are missin'. How did dey get out wit'out de cameras seein' dem? I doan like it, no' one little bit. It reeks of dark magic. They've been gone for hours now, and Zeke is goin' out of his mind. No' dat I blame him. Losing one child is bad enough, but to lose t'ree in less den a week? I can't imagine wha' he's going t'rough.

We've swept de grounds and looked in ever' room in de plantation house. Dey be nowhere.

"Where the hell have you been?" Zeke snarls. "We've been calling you for hours."

Mary and I jump at de accusation in his voice, but it's no' us he's growlin' at. It's de damn demon who's been MIA for days.

"I was trying to find everything we need to locate Emma Rose." Silas is unperturbed. "I had to…" It's only then he notices the vibe of the room. "What's happened?"

"What's happened?" Zeke looks ready to do the demon serious harm. "What's happened is she wasn't on the damn island, and now Dan and Eric have gone missing. *That's what's happened!*"

"I knew she wouldn't be on the island. That's why I went searching for this spell. No one would go to the one place we'd look for them first."

How he can be smug wit' ever'tin dat's going on around us is crazy.

"Can you find Dan?" Zeke asks, his fists clenching. He has to be restrainin' himself to keep from harmin' de demon.

"Dan is not my priority right now. My granddaughter must be found. We can locate the missing children later."

He takes the bag he's holding over to de table and begins pulling t'ings out. "This spell should get around anything that is blocking us from finding our darling girl. I've been assured it will get past the most ancient of spells."

"Assured by who?" I ask, no' trusting de demon at all.

"Those who know about these things," Silas answers. He starts mixing t'ings in a silver bowl and speaking in a language so ancient, I doubt it's ever been spoken in de presence of humans before.

He pulls out a knife that's made out of what looks like bone and slices it across his palm, letting it drip into the mixture. A puff of smoke curls up from the bowl. Silas passes the knife to Zeke, who doesn't hesitate to slice his palm. The knife is held out to me, and I falter. I don't want my blood near the demon.

"He won't touch your blood, Cass. I promise." Zeke waits me out.

"I doan want him to do de spell."

"He doesn't have to. You or I can do it."

Silas wisely doesn't say a word. Instead, he begins drawing the outline of a circle.

"What sort of spell is dis?" I ask.

"It'll find your sister." Silas stands when he's done. "That's all you need to know, my darling boy."

"No, demon, dat's no' all I need to know." I gesture to the circle. "Dat looks like a summoning circle."

Silas presses his lips together.

"Silas, you need to tell us the truth."

"It is a summoning circle to hold one of the oldest demons in Hell. He is the only one with enough juice to get to Emma Rose through the kind of shield she has around her."

"I'm no' summoning a demon." No way. Emma wouldn't want me to either.

"Even if it means we can't find your sister any other way?"

"Emma wou' be de first to say hell no."

"She wouldn't say 'hell' at all," Zeke says. "He's right, though. She would never allow this. You should have told us from the beginning what was going on, Silas. We wouldn't have agreed to it."

"I know." He flicks his hand toward both of us, and I'm frozen. Ice encases my feet and my arms. It's even snared itself over my mouth, cutting off my objections. The demon picks up the bowl and the knife. "You had the chance to do this yourself, boy, but you've left me no choice. I will not let your morals cost my granddaughter her life. Yours or your father's."

My eyes cut to Zeke, who is in de same position as I am, only he's pissed. I've never seen him so angry before. His eyes have gone ice cold, and dey be scarier den de demon in front of me.

Silas cuts deeply into my palm, and my blood drips down to add to de mixture. A loud whistle goes t'rough de air, and yellow smoke billows up from de bowl. Silas sets candles around de circle and lights dem.

He sets de bowl down in de middle of de circle and steps away, speaking once again in dat language I have never heard.

The lights flicker, and de floor rocks beneath us as he keeps talking, his arms raising over his head, his voice growing louder and louder.

De whole house shakes, and dey be loud knocks on de door, Zeke's fa'der demandin' to know wha's going on. None of us pay him much mind, dou. Our eyes are locked on de huge form amassin' in de circle, a circle I personally doan t'ink is stable enough to hold dis monster demon.

The demon who materializes is one dat nightmares are made of. He is big, so big he makes de room feel claustrophobic. His face is no' really a face, but a collection of parts. His body is animalistic, and he snorts, his gaze settling on Silas.

"Why have you summoned me?" His voice is ancient and painful to the eardrums.

"I am looking for someone who has been hidden from us through magic. A magic so old and powerful we can't break the spell. We need you to find her."

"And what will you give me for this

request?" His black eyes flicker to Zeke and me, where we are frozen in the ice.

With a flick of his hand, we're free from de ice. I stumble, but Zeke doesn't. I'm guessin' dis is no' de first time he's been a victim of de ice.

"They are not on the menu."

A rumble comes from the beast. "A reaper and an Angel. It would be a nice payment."

"I'm offering you your freedom in exchange for the girl's location."

Zeke starts to say something, but I see his lips disappear. Silas silenced him wit'out even looking. I understand Zeke's fear. Lettin' som'tin dis old an dis evil loose is no' a good idea.

"Think about it, Azazoul. You won't have to return to the pit. You will be free to walk this world. Is that not worth the information on one insignificant human?"

"How can you promise this, demon? I am shackled to my prison cell."

"You're here, aren't you?" Silas counters.

The demon grunts. "Who is dis girl?"

Silas picks up a picture of Emma off

Zeke's desk and shows it to the demon. "Her name is Emma Crane, but she was known before as Mattie Hathaway. She's been missing for a week."

The demon's black eyes roll back, and all dat is left is a milky white eye socket. He looks even more terrifyin' like dis.

"The girl is moving from place to place, traveling. She keeps returning to one place…to your hole, demon. She will return there again."

"What do you mean, she's moving?" Silas looks disturbed. "I have been in my hole for two days, and she's not been there."

The creature shrugs. "It is what I see."

"Azazoul, thank you for your information. As agreed upon, the price is your freedom. If you drink from the bowl inside the circle, it will free you from your prison. It will also protect this house. You may not return here or harm anyone on these premises. You may not harm the girl you found. Do you agree?"

"For my freedom? Aye, demon. I agree."

"Then drink."

The big, lumbering body leans down and grips the bowl in its massive hands and tips it back, slurping the contents inside. His eyes flash with that same yellow smoke from earlier, and then he's gone.

"What did you do?" I whisper.

"Found your sister."

"But at what price? What is that thing?"

"Something that will never harm you."

Zeke stalks toward Silas, who still has no lips.

"You goin' to fix dat?"

The demon rolls his eyes, and Zeke's mouth reappears.

"You let a Fallen loose from his prison? Do you understand what you have done?"

"You did wha'?" My eyes widen. He let loose a Fallen Angel?

"Not just any old Fallen, but one the others considered so dangerous he needed to be housed in an unbreakable jail."

"We need allies in the fight against the Fallen, Ezekiel. They're coming for her sooner rather than later. I'd rather have one on our side, and it doesn't hurt that he's one they're afraid of."

"You fool. You made a deal. The deal is done. He owes us no allegiance."

"You don't know how demons think. This will matter to him."

"I…"

A growl so menacing it raises the hairs on every inch of my body reverberates through the house.

"Wha' the hell is dat?" I run for de door, yanking it open. Josiah is at de end of the hall where the back stairs are. He's looking up, confused.

"One of the shifters has shifted. He's pacing in the hall."

De same growl is ripped from de shifter, only dis time he sounds more like he's challenging something. Giving de old man no time to ask any more questions, I take de stairs two at a time until I come face to face wit' wha' de shifter is growling at.

A hulking figure is perched a few feet away from him. It's almost like a big bird, but its talons are lethal looking. I've never seen any'tin like it before.

Thank God I have my blessed blade. It's small enough dat I carry it with me. It's more of a dagger den a sword, dou. It may be small, but it be let'al. It took Uncle Rob a lot to get dis for us. Havin' only one was a pain.

Approaching de rabid shifter slowly, I stop about a foot from him so he can scent de air. I doan need him attackin' me. Amber eyes glare up at me, but I make no aggressive move. He turns his attention back to de thing at de end of de hallway.

The door de shifter is in front of opens, and Ava Malone steps out into de hallway de same time de bird t'ing launches. De shifter growls and shoves de girl inside, twisting in time to catch de bird before it can reach her. An awful sound comes out of it as dey struggle. Ava slams de door, and it pushes me into action. Leaping on de t'ing's back, I stab it with de dagger as de shifter's teeth sink into its neck.

De bird does not give up. It t'rows us off and den shakes like a dog wou' after it's gotten wet. It's hawkish gaze lands on de door, and it charges, but de shifter is moving faster den light. It jumps and knocks de bird away from the door, taking a lot of damage from its talons.

Getting up, I run to help de big wolf who is getting his ass beat, but he's not giving up. Whoever he is, he's taking protecting Ava dead serious. She's lucky he was up here.

While de bird is focusing all its attention on de shifter, it gives me de opportunity to slide my blade in de side of its neck, nickin' wha' I hope is an artery. Pullin' de blade out, I keep stabbing it anywhere I can get purchase, ignoring the painful cries of de shifter. He's keepin' it busy so I can do dis. I doan need to be a mind reader to know dat.

It takes several more stabs of de blade into de t'ing's neck before it gives a painful shudder and falls, its talons releasing de shifter, who doesn't move. He just whimpers. I push de bird off him and bend down. He's ripped to shreds.

Footsteps sound behind me, and I turn to see Caleb and James Malone runnin' up de stairs, both of dem holdin' guns. When did Caleb start carryin' a gun?

"What's going on?" James rushes over and opens Ava's door. She's standing there, the base of the lamp in her hands. "Are you okay?"

She nods and peers around James, a gasp falling from her lips. "Oh, no!" Pushing past her father, she comes to kneel beside me. "Is he okay?"

"I doan know. I'm no' sure wha' dat creature is, so I doan know wha' dis damage will do to him."

"He protected me." Her hand comes out hesitantly and strokes the wolf's tattered ear. "Thank you."

The wolf whines, his breathing shallow.

"Can you shift?" I ask him.

My only answer is a painful whine.

"Where's Sabien?" Maybe de witch will know wha' to do.

"He's outside searching for Dan and Eric." Ezekiel pulls out his phone and shoots off a text. "Hopefully, he's not too far away and will come running when he hears his nephew has been injured. Cass,

Caleb, can you give me a hand with him? We'll get him moved back into his room. Papa, can you deal with that thing?" Zeke motions to the big bird.

"How did that get in the house?" James asks, pulling his daughter up and out of the way.

"It piggybacked off a summoned demon." Zeke assumes de most risk and grips de shifter's head while Caleb slides his hands under de shifter's back, and I pick up de rear. De sound dat comes out of de animal is one I hope to never hear again when we move him down de hall to his bedroom. Now dat I know de shifter is related to de Blackburnes, I'm hoping dey migh' know wha' to do for him. If he can't shift, he can't heal.

"Cass, is there a local alpha who might be able to come and force him to shift and heal?" Zeke opens the adjoining bathroom door and pulls a bucket out from under de sink. He fills it with warm water then does his best to clean de wolf's wounds. It is no' something I would have expected him to do.

"I can make a call." Last time I was

anywhere near de wolf shifters, Emma about got us turned into dog food. Not sure they'll come anywhere near de Cranes, dou, even if Emma hadn't caused problems before. No one in de community trusts Ezekiel Crane.

"Is there anything I can do to help?" Ava asks from de doorway.

"Do you want to help me clean his wounds?"

She nods, and Zeke motions to the bathroom for her to get another washcloth.

"I'll go make dat call."

I step out of de room and bypass the Malones and Josiah, who are poking at de bird creature. My mind shies away from dat and how I played an unwillin' part in bringin' it here. Dat is a problem for ano'der day. Right now, we have enough to deal wit'. Emma, Dan, and Eric missing. A Blackburne injured.

We have more den enough to deal wit'.

Emma/Mattie

The Red Church
New Orleans, LA

Something drew me here. A sense of power that called to me. I don't know what it is, but it's always called to me, and I followed it. If I go near people now, I might hurt them. Deep down, I know that wouldn't be good, even though in my present state of mind, I don't really care. The part of my soul that still remains does.

Why am I here, though? I wander through the halls, into the kitchens, and then up the spiral staircase to the rounded room at the top and look out over the trees. Their branches are empty and barren, resembling skeletal hands reaching and bending in the wind.

We haven't started construction on the place yet, just secured it against the elements and had a cleaning crew come in and do a deep clean.

Though why this is what I'm thinking about right now makes no sense to me. Perhaps because it's mundane? My feelings have been cut off, and I'm numb. Even the rage has gone. I guess it makes sense I'd be thinking about unimportant things.

"Rose?"

Rhea is standing a few feet away, looking concerned. I'm covered in blood—drenched in it, really. I'm sure I look like I'm playing the part of Carrie in that old horror movie where she's standing on stage, covered in blood, and she snaps, killing everyone in the gym.

"We've been looking for you." She takes a few steps closer.

"Don't," I whisper. "I might hurt you."

She stops.

"You can't hurt me, sweetheart."

"I could."

She shakes her head. "Why are you here?"

"I don't know. This place called to me, and I came."

"How did you get here?"

"I don't know. I just thought about it, and here I was."

"Where is Kristoff?"

I shrug. "Don't know, but I killed the others."

"The others?"

"I killed them all."

Her eyes widen, and she takes a few more steps closer. My hands blaze to life with fire. I don't want her to come closer to me.

"Sweetheart, I'm not going to hurt you."

"No one will ever hurt me again."

Real alarm flares in her eyes. I sound dead to myself, so I'm sure she's panicking.

"What happened, Rose?"

"They're dead."

"Who's dead?"

"Dan and Eric. I killed them."

"What?" she whispers.

"Dan's dead because of me, but I killed Eric with my bare hands. They're dead. I should be dead too. I would be dead if you hadn't done this to me."

"Rose, my protections won't save you from the bond you and Dan share. Are you sure he's dead?"

"I felt it."

She frowns, but she wasn't there. She didn't feel the loss rip through me, didn't feel my body try to die with him.

I couldn't save them, but maybe there is one thing I can do.

"How do I find where they're keeping Kane?"

"I don't know, Rose. We're not allowed near the reapers."

"I looked in The Between, but I found nothing."

"The reapers have their own home. The Between is just a passageway from this plane to the next."

"Then how do I find their home?"

"Gods and goddesses are not allowed

there, Rose. You would die."

"But I'm not just part god, am I? I'm a reaper." And if I die, I die. I don't care.

"Rose…"

"No, you will tell me." I put every ounce of control and power I have in my Voice. The way Zeke taught me. "How do I get to the reapers' homeworld?"

She blinks rapidly like she's fighting her answer, but it comes out anyway. "You have to travel through a portal."

"Where is this portal?"

"We're standing on one."

"What?"

"This church was built on a nexus of power, one that houses a portal for the gods. We are the only ones who can use it. It was built by us. It's why this place calls to you, why it's always called to you. It's part of you."

Well, that explains that. I never understood why I loved this place, why I was compelled to buy it for The Hathaway Foundation's corporate office. Now I know. It's as much a part of me as Rhea or Silas is.

"Show me."

"Rose, you need to think about this…"

"No, I don't. I need to find Kane. He's being punished because of me, and I won't leave him there."

Maybe my emotions aren't as tamped down as I thought because anger surges at the idea of Kane held somewhere, being tortured. I can't leave him there if I can help it. I know what it's like to be helpless, and it's not a good feeling.

Rhea nods and motions me to follow her. We go back down the stairs and out the side door. There's a cellar door I hadn't paid much attention to. My first thought had been snakes, and I wasn't touching that mess with a ten-foot pole.

Of course it's where she goes. Once we're down the stairs, she places her hand on the wall, and the entire place lights up with a soft golden glow.

"Come, Rose." She reaches for me, and I back away. "Don't touch me."

Instead of arguing, she moves deeper into the cellar until she comes to the very back. Placing her hand on the wall once more, the old stones begin to move and shift until they form a doorway. Very much like the effect in the *Harry Potter* movies when Hagrid opened the doorway to Diagon Alley. It's actually a really cool effect in person. And it gets cooler when the inside of the door begins to glow with the same golden color of Rhea's eyes.

"This is the doorway between worlds. There are a few on every world, known only to our kind, and it is a secret that must be kept between us. No one else must know. Not Ezekiel, not Silas, not Dan. No one, Rose. You must swear it."

"I swear, no one will know about this place."

"Now that you know where this is, and you own the property, it is your responsibility. You are the guardian of this gateway. Do you understand, Rose?"

"Yes."

"Place your hand here, and I will release it into your care."

"Are you its guardian?"

"No one is. It has been unattended for a millennium."

I place my hand on the spot she indicated, and bright golden light flares, engulfing me in this warm glow. It thaws the cold that has taken over my mind, and I fall, the pain of Dan's and Eric's deaths almost crippling me. No. I can't...I claw my way back to that cold, empty place.

"Rose," Rhea whispers, her own pain apparent.

"How do I find Kane from here?" I ask instead of taking her up on the opportunity to talk.

"Simply open up your reaping abilities, tell the door where you wish to go, and walk through."

I can do that.

"Be specific, Rose. If not, you could end up somewhere you do not wish to be."

I remember what happened to Harry when he traveled through the fireplace. He wasn't clear, and it ended up badly for him.

Standing, I close my eyes and imagine Kane. I see him as he appears to me simply because I don't know what his true form looks like. I remember our friendship, all the times he's helped me until I have a good sense of him.

"Take me to the reaper Kane."

I say it clearly and concisely before stepping through the doorway.

Vertigo hits, and I close my eyes as I'm sucked through time and space. It's like something is trying to pull my insides out through my nose.

When I come to a standstill, I take several deep breaths and open my eyes, leery of where I might have ended up.

I'm in a room that smells very much like a mixture of blood and urine. It's a distinct odor, but yet it's not the same either. This isn't metallic. It's more of a juicy, slimy stink. It's gross.

My gaze falls onto the wall where there are dozens of knives and other instruments hung. Most of them are dripping with a blue goo. Double gross.

And then I see him.

Only it's not the Kane I know. His face is gaunt and foreign, the mask of a skull that isn't quite human. His body is tall and thin, bleeding from more wounds than I can count. And he's chained to the corner.

"Kane?" I whisper.

He looks up and flinches.

I approach him like I would a wounded animal. "Kane, it's Emma. I'm here to take you home."

He shakes his head, his gaze focused behind me, and I whirl to see another reaper standing there. He's as tall as Deleriel, who was over seven feet.

"You're not supposed to be here." The voice is alien and hollow. "Why are you here?"

"I'm here for Kane."

"You are not allowed. No one is allowed here."

"Too bad. I'm here, and I'm taking him with me."

"Who are you, child, and how did you get here?"

"I'm Emma Mattie Hathaway Crane, and I'm here because this is where Kane is."

"Crane…you are the daughter of Rhea."

"I am."

"You should be dead. Gods and goddesses are not allowed within my prison. Anywhere near the Reaper's Hall.

You should have been stricken dead the moment you crossed into our homeworld."

"I'm not just a goddess, though. I'm part reaper. I have just as much right to be here as you do."

He tilts his head, thinking about that little nugget of information. "Aye, child, you do have a right to the reaper's homeworld of Attrax, but you cannot be here. This is a prison for those who have betrayed our purpose."

"You mean because Kane helped me when he should have been off collecting souls?"

"You were the one he ignored his duties for?"

"Yes."

He shakes his head. "You are young, a new reaper. He should have been teaching you how to be a reaper instead of helping you do whatever frivolous things you were doing."

"I was saving people's lives. I don't call that frivolous."

"Life is not our concern." Wisdom shines in his voice. "We are keepers of

279

souls. Our duty is to be there to help them pass from one plane to the next. We protect them. They are our purpose. Kane did not teach you this?"

I'm sure he did, but I don't remember most things he tried to teach me. I didn't want to be a reaper, and I hid from it.

"I'm not dead, and the living are very much my responsibility."

"But they are not Kane's. Souls were devoured because he put his allegiance to you over his own sworn duty. Are those souls any less important than your human lives just because they no longer have bodies?"

Perhaps if my emotions weren't so cut off, his words might matter to me, but in this state of mind, I don't care.

"And are those human lives any less important just because they are alive?" I counter.

He steps closer. "I can't smell anything about you that is human, child. You are in a human body, but you're as cold and dead as I am."

I smile. "I know."

"Perhaps we can talk. Will you let me

escort you to a safe place here on our world?"

"I came for Kane."

"He's being punished, child. He's not going anywhere."

The reaper idly picks up a blade and examines it. Kane flinches away from him.

"He's coming with me."

A sigh leaves the creature. "I have no wish to harm you. But if you insist on this course of action, you will leave me with no choice."

Shaking my head, I turn to go to Kane, and in the next instant, I'm slammed into the wall by an ice-cold wind.

"You will leave now."

I'm sick and tired of getting attacked. I throw my own reaper wind at him, and he lands just as hard against the other wall.

"I don't want to kill you either, old one, but I will if you try to stop me."

"You can't kill me. I'm immortal."

"Tell that to Deleriel or the blood demon I killed." I smile my most sharkish smile. "I have no problems killing you."

"Foolish little reaper." His rasp fills the air as he starts toward me. "I warned you to leave, and now you will be punished for defying me."

"I'm not the foolish one. You are." My hands ignite with glowing balls of blue fire. The flames are tinged with the golden light of my mother's heritage. "I am Death."

And with that, I unleash the fire onto the ancient reaper. His scream is long and loud as his body withers in the fire surrounding him. It takes no effort, really.

Once I'm satisfied he's gone, I turn back to Kane, who is staring at me in something akin to horror.

"What happened to you?" he asks, his own ancient voice weak.

"Nothing good." It takes barely anything to break the chains on his wrists and ankles. "Can you walk?"

He shakes his head.

"I'll carry you, then." He's awkward to hold because of my broken bones, but thanks to my demon half, I'm strong enough to carry him. "Now, where's the danged door?"

I forgot to ask Rhea about that.

Well, it's here somewhere…or is it inside me? I took ownership of the door. Maybe it'll open for me. I concentrate on the wall and form the door in my mind, projecting its image on the stones, and sure enough, it appears.

"Take me to Silas's studio."

That same vertigo hits me as I step through the door, but it's easier to manage. When I end up in Silas's studio, I smile. That was almost too easy.

"Was there just the one reaper guarding you?" I ask as an afterthought.

"Yes, but many come throughout the day. They'll know I'm gone soon."

"They won't look for you here." I walk down the hallway and into my bedroom. "What can I get you? What do you need to heal?"

"Rest, Emma. I need rest. My body doesn't require food or water. It just needs time to heal."

"Then you take all the time you need to rest. I'll come check on you later. I have one more thing to attend to."

"Emma?" He reaches out his skeletal hand, and I take it without hesitation. "Thank you for coming for me."

"You're family, Kane. Family will always protect family. You don't have to thank me. I'm the reason you were there to begin with. I'm sorry I'm the cause of your pain."

"I did what I did because I wanted to. Don't blame yourself, and don't try to fight all the reapers, eh?"

"Don't worry about it, Kane. Just rest." I pull a throw over his frame. He looks frail and thin. "Sleep. You're safe now."

I wait until his eyes close and he appears to be breathing deeply before I go back home.

To deal with Kristoff.

I materialize in front of Zeke's plantation. Everything is eerily quiet outside. There are no cars in the driveway. Is everyone gone? Maybe out looking for me?

"Peaches, bring him to me."

I started to kill him outright, but it's not my decision. Or at least not entirely. That warmth from before snuck into my plans, and I decided to ask Cass what we should do with the vampire. It is, after all, Alice who stands to lose her life.

The hulking Hellhound bounds into view, the vampire in her massive maw. He's wounded, and I have to wonder if Alice feels his wounds like Dan does mine. Or did.

No. Can't go there.

Peaches drops him at my feet like a cat would if she was out hunting for her human and delivered her prize. It's cute. I rub her jaw then bend down to look at Kristoff.

"I told you I'd get loose and you'd die screaming. I meant that."

He spits blood out of his mouth. "I always win."

"We'll see." Grabbing him by the hair, I drag him up the porch steps and into the house.

The house is not quiet on the inside. I hear feet pounding upstairs and lots of noise coming from Papa's den. That is where I go first.

I catch a glimpse of myself in the mirror. I'm covered in blood. My bones are broken, the evidence in the bulges along my bruised body evident. The way my head's tilted and my stuttered moves remind me of the protection demon who once came for me. That thing scared the bejesus out of me, and the image of myself gives me the same freaking heebie-jeebies.

"Emma Rose?"

My head swivels in the direction of my grandfather's voice. His expression would be almost amusing if I wasn't in a homicidal mood.

"I need Cass."

He takes a step away from me and calls, "Zeke, Cass! Come down here right now."

There's a pounding on the stairs, and my father comes into view. He's not horrified by my appearance. He's relieved. I'm glad I'm not feeling anything right now. His pain would sway me from what I'm going to do.

"Emma Rose?" Zeke whispers, and I jerk away from him when he tries to hug me.

"Don't touch me."

"Doan touch her." Cass appears out of my dad's office. "She's not de Emma we know. She's de o'der Emma right now."

"The other Emma?" Zeke asks, the need to hold me written all over his face.

"De Emma who killed a Fallen Angel. She had to cut herself off. She's not feelin' any'tin right now o'der den homicidal rage. You touch her, and you might die. She'd regret it later, but she won't righ' now."

"How do you know that?" Josiah asks, coming to stand by Zeke.

"I've been in dat place once, de nigh' my parents died. I went dere to keep from feeling any'tin, and it works, but you have no conscience there. Leave de girl alone until she decides to come back from dere."

"I don't know if that's possible anymore."

"It is, Emma. I promise." His gaze lands on Kristoff. "Why is he no' dead?"

"Because it has to be your choice."

"My choice?"

"He made Alice his human servant. I kill him, and she dies."

"Lies. We wou' know…"

"Call Alice. Ask her how she's feeling. He's healing rapidly, and I think he's pulling that from her."

Cass takes out his phone and does exactly that. When he finishes his call, he looks up, bleak. "She's in a lot of pain, she's bleedin', and she shouldn't be bleedin'."

"What do you want to do, Cass? We can't let him go."

"We found them!" Nathaniel bursts through the front door, along with the Blackburne crew. They're helping Dan and Eric through the door.

No.

No.

No.

They're dead.

Dead.

Dead.

Dead.

I glare down at Kristoff. "What tricks are you playing at?"

"I told you I always win."

Dan's eyes are on me, Luca supporting him. He looks half-dead, but I'm half-dead. If it weren't for the demon blood, I'd probably be dead.

"Sweetheart...I..."

"No. You're dead. I saw you die. Ralph killed you. He slit your throat, and I couldn't save you. You're dead. This is a trick. Kristoff is in my head, and this is a trick."

I center all my confusion and rage at Dan, and I imagine his heart in my hands. I squeeze, and he wheezes. His legs buckle, and he falls to the floor, holding his chest.

"Hathaway…stop. It's really Dan. It's not a trick. I promise."

"You're dead too. I killed you. Ripped your head off. You're both dead, and it's all my fault."

Alex Reed steps away from the group and eases her way up to me. "Listen to me, Emma. This isn't a trick. I know how you're feeling. Remember what my grandfather did to me, and I had to choose which reality was real? Now you have to choose. If you do this, Dan will die. You'll die, and Kristoff wins. That man you're killing is Dan. You have to choose Dan."

She places her hand on me, and something happens. I hear locks opening in my mind, and those doors are blown wide open. Power rushes through me, and Kristoff screams beneath me. My hands are glowing embers of golden light.

They're burning him.

The warmth of that glow flows through every cell in my body, knitting together my broken bones and making me whole. It flows into Alex, and I feel doors in her mind as well, doors I can unlock. She's broken. I feel it. I can heal her and let my light flood through her, healing her and opening locks.

She gasps and staggers away from me. Luca catches her before she falls. "What did you do to her?"

"I healed her." I turn my attention back to Dan. I'm still squeezing his heart. Choose to let him live or not. I can't live in a reality without him, but I saw him die. I felt it. I felt my body start to die, but my rage kept me alive.

This has to be a trick. Kristoff is orchestrating it. He's stopped screaming. His face is blackened and blistered from the burns, but he's still smiling.

I hate him.

My rage rushes back and funnels directly into him. His bones crush, and his screams fill my heart with utter joy. I watch as his blood begins to seep out of

291

every pore in his body. I break him until he's on the verge of death and then pull him back.

The shifter in me howls, and my hands morph once more into claws. Smiling, I straddle the vampire. "I told you that you would die screaming." My claws tear into him, shredding skin, bone, and muscle. More screams echo through the manor, and I laugh. His pain makes me so happy.

"No, Emma, stop." Cass is right beside me. He knows better than to touch me. "You're killing Alice, Emma. Please stop."

"I'll heal her." There's no real emotion in my voice.

"Her bro'der is on de phone, Emma. She's dying. You have to stop. Please. She's my best friend. I can't lose her."

I don't want to stop. "You don't know what he did to me, what he made me do to Eric." Kristoff deserves to die.

"Emma Rose, you need to stop this." Zeke tries to grab me, and I shove him away. He slams against the wall, his head bouncing hard. I hear the crack and heal him before it even starts to cause him problems.

Dan gurgles and falls over. He's almost gone.

"Mathilda Louise Hathaway, what are you doing?"

"Mama?" I whisper.

"Stop this right now."

"You're not here. You're not real."

I refuse to believe what's right in front of me. Kristoff has used Mama against me before. He'd try to use her again if it meant I stopped and he got to live.

"Go away. You're not real."

I turn back to Kristoff and sink my claws into the flesh of his stomach and tear, pulling his intestines out. The smell is delicious, like a well-cooked steak.

"Hilda."

Eli? I thought he left me when Dan came.

I turn my head to see him standing beside my mama. "Eli?"

"Hilda, you have to stop. You can't kill him. Cass will never forgive you if Alice dies."

"He deserves worse than what I'm going to do to him."

"I know, but you can't, Hilda." He nudges my mother. "Do you want your mama to see what you've become when she risked everything to keep you safe?"

"Did you bring her here?"

He nods.

"She's real?"

"Yes, Hilda, she's real."

Mama smiles. Eli brought her to me, but I don't know why. "Why did you bring her here?"

"Because you need her, Hilda. The Cranes and Silas will tell you it's okay, that what you're about to do is for the best. Everyone else will understand because you aren't you right now. Dan will die. Maybe you will too. But the one person who won't let you believe this is okay, that it's who you are, is your mother. She raised you to be a kind, loving person. She sacrificed your life to save you. She's not going to let you go to a place you'll never come back from. I told you to be Mattie Hathaway, to be that cold girl, and you did that. You escaped. You made Ralph pay. Kristoff will pay. You can't be that girl anymore,

Hilda. You have to walk away from all that cold darkness. You survived."

"I don't know how to do that."

"I know, and that's why Claire is here. She's the reason for every ounce of goodness in you. She's here to remind you of that little girl who loved bigger and harder than anyone else. Let her bring you back, Hilda. Let her bring Emma back."

Mama holds her arms open, her face forgiving and full of acceptance. I want to be the person I was becoming. I don't like this person. I hate her, really, but she's necessary. She keeps me alive. I don't want to forget her any more than I want to be her.

Eli's right about one thing. It was Mama who showed me how to be kind. Even when she was high as a kite, she was always nice to everyone. She never had an unkind word for anyone. It was Mama who gave me my moral compass, who taught me right from wrong. She wasn't perfect—far from it—but she is the reason I had any kindness in me after foster care.

"I hated you," I tell her, my voice fierce. The cold I'm surrounded in makes me able to say this to her. "I hated you for murdering me. I still do."

And that's the truth. I forgave her, but I hate her.

"I know, Mattie. I know you hate me. I don't blame you. What I did is unforgivable. I thought it was the only way to protect you. I was drugged up and hallucinating. All I've ever wanted to do was to keep you safe. I'm sorry for the pain that brought you. I'm sorry I left you all alone. I'm sorry for what happened to you after I died. I'm so, so sorry, baby girl. I couldn't help you then, but I can help you now if you let me. This isn't you."

"It is me," I rebuke her. "I was born to be this person. Cultivated through manipulation and magic for hundreds of years. I was born to be a killer."

"That may be so, but you don't have to give in to it. We are the choices we make, no more, no less. If you choose to be a killer, then that's who you'll be. If you choose to be the woman I raised you to be, then that's who you'll be. The choice is and always has been yours, baby girl."

Everything in me wants to murder Kristoff for all the pain he caused me, for the women he killed, for all the people he harmed or destroyed who I don't know about. I can do it so easily. I glance over at my father, and his face is a mask of pain and worry. Mama's right. He'll tell me I did what I had to do. Cass is sitting right beside me. He'll hate me. He's my brother, and he'll end up hating me before we even get a chance.

Do I choose to be the cold killer sitting here or to be the kind woman who was becoming the sort of person who deserved the love of someone like Dan Richards?

I look to him next. He's on the floor, one hand reaching out to me, the other on his chest. He's dying. I'm killing him. But he's already dead. I felt him die.

Or did I?

Was it just another trick of Kristoff's?

I always win.

Is this what he meant? Am I so twisted around that I can't recognize the truth?

Is this the truth?

Is Dan real?

Or is it Kristoff in my head?

Is any of this real?

I don't know.

"Please, Mattie, let me help you."

Mama's arms are wide open.

I need help to walk away from the cold, white place. I need help to find my way back.

I need help.

Dropping Kristoff's arm, I stand and stagger away from him.

"It's okay, Mattie," Eli reassures me. "What is my job as your Guardian Angel?"

"To be what I need."

"And what do you need?"

"I need help."

"Don't I always know how to help you?"

I nod.

"Then trust me. Trust your mama."

Nodding, I take a hesitant step toward her and then another until I'm running. As soon as I hit her, she enfolds me into her arms, and the cold surrounding me doesn't disappear as I expected. I'm not magically healed of it. It's there, but I can breathe now. I'm not blinded by the cold. I understand a little better what I was doing.

"I don't know how to come back from this."

"I know, baby girl. First, you need to release Dan before you kill him."

Without a thought, my hand stops squeezing his heart, and I hear him coughing. Maybe he's real, maybe he's not, but there is one simple truth that I couldn't see before. Dan is mine, and I'll protect him with my dying breath, even from myself. Real or not, I can't kill him. Killing him a second time would be more than I can handle.

"Good girl." Mama strokes my hair.

"I missed you," I whisper softly. "I hate you, but I missed you."

"I know, baby girl. Mama missed you too." She hugs me tight, and in her hold, some of that cold rage cools, disappearing and letting my mind clear a little more. "It's okay. Mama's here, baby. Mama's here."

We sink to our knees, and for the first time since I was in that basement room, I let myself cry. Hard sobs break out of me, and I hold my mama tight as the pain and the anger empty out of my mind. I'm not saying I'm back to myself. I'm still in that cold, empty place in my mind, but some of my emotions are leaking through, ripping holes into my solace.

"There's my girl. It's okay, sweetheart. I promise it's okay."

"Is he all right?" I ask and glance to where Dan is just getting back up. He's sitting, one knee up, the other leg thrown out. His color is better. Is he real? Will he forgive me if he is?

I only see the woman sneaking up behind Dan because I'm looking directly at him. She has a knife in her hand. What is she doing?

No. The knife is right there. She can't. Not again. This can't be happening again.

I always win. I can hear Kristoff laughing in my head.

"Stop."

"I can't." She yanks Dan's head back and puts the knife to his throat. "I have to do this."

Kristoff laughs as Mrs. Banks begins to glide the blade across Dan's throat. "I told you I always win."

Real or not, no one hurts him.

I don't want to do this, but I have to.

He's mine.

The blade flies out of her and directly into her heart. I thrust it deep. I just have to think about it to make it happen. She stumbles back then falls.

Everyone is silent.

I killed her.

My body shakes harder, and the tears roll down my face. Dan looks between me and Mrs. Banks, his deep brown eyes as horrified as I'm feeling.

I killed Mrs. B.

I killed her.

I killed her.

Dan crawls over to me, and the moment his skin touches mine, I know he's real. He's as real as everyone standing there looking at me.

Eric walks slowly over to where I'm huddled against my mama. His blue eyes are electric. He's always had the most beautiful eyes. "Hathaway, I'm not dead."

He holds out his hand, and I take it.

He's real. He's not a figment of my imagination. He's real.

But Mrs. Banks is dead.

And I killed her.

The room springs into action. People swarm Mrs. B, and they pick her up, carrying her into the kitchen. I see the reaper walking with her. Soon her soul will leave her body, and she'll go with the reaper. I could stop it, but I'm afraid to. What if pulling her back causes one of us to die like Meg did? I won't risk Eric, Mary, Ethan, Dan, or Nathaniel. Or Cass.

My brother.

I sweep my gaze to where he's standing. He looks shellshocked. I can't blame him.

"Cass?"

"Yeah?"

"You okay?"

"No."

"Are we okay?"

"I doan know if I'm okay wit' any'tin, but I'm no' runnin' from you if dat be wha' you be askin'."

"It is what I'm asking."

"You did wha' you had to do to protect your man. I wou' have done de same if it were you or Caryle or Rob. I understand, Emma."

Dan pulls me from my mama and into his lap. It's the one place that is better than my mama's arms.

"It's okay, baby. I got you now, Squirt."

Squirt.

The other Dan never called me that.

"You were dead. You were both dead." I latch on to him and snuggle my nose into the side of his neck, breathing in his woodsy smell as deeply as I can. "I'm so sorry, Dan, so sorry. I thought you and Eric were another trick Kristoff was playing. I didn't mean to hurt you. I'm so sorry."

"It's okay, baby. I'm okay. We're okay. Remember, I'm in it for the long haul."

That causes me to cry harder.

"Shhh, baby, it's okay now."

"Why is there a bleeding reaper in your

room?" Silas asks as he strolls in.

"It's Kane. I needed to hide him."

Silas pulls me away from Dan and almost crushes me. "The next time you get ideas about turning yourself over to a psychopath, you are going on my rack, my darling girl. That's a promise."

He's shaking. That's how I know how afraid he is. Silas loves me in his own psychopathic way. The only person allowed to hurt me is him, and I know every time he's had to, it's hurt him deeply to do so.

"I love you, Silas."

He goes completely still.

"I love you too, my darling girl."

Smiling, I hug him tighter and then look for my papa. His judgement is one I'm dreading. He's standing there, staring off into space. God only knows what's going through his head.

"Papa?"

His gaze snaps to me.

There is torment there. He loved Mrs. Banks like his own sister. She was family. I hate that I'm the one who killed her, but I had to. Kristoff was in her head, and I had no control over the situation. I knew if I didn't kill her, she'd find a way to hurt Dan. I felt it in my bones. I saw it. Somehow, I saw her hurting him until he died. It was a flash of images. I'm not sure how that happened. I haven't had a vision since Eli died.

"I'm so sorry, Papa." My head hangs down, ashamed. I chose Dan over Mrs. Banks. I'll always choose him. It might not be right, but that's how it is.

He seems to snap out of his funk and steps away from the wall, and Silas passes me to him.

"Don't, *ma petite*. Do not blame yourself. Mrs. Banks was family, but you're my daughter. I will always side with you. You did what must be done. I love you, Emma Rose."

"I love you too, Papa, and I'm so very sorry."

"Shh." He strokes my sticky, bloody hair. "It's okay, *ma petite*. We have you. You're safe."

Silas produces a vial and pushes it at me. "Dead man's blood. We need to get the vampire out of your head."

I drink it without a quibble. I'm not a fan of drinking blood. It feels like a blasphemy to me since the Bible strictly says not to drink the blood, for the blood is the life.

"I have to go now, Hilda."

I look over to see him hovering beside us. Those aqua eyes of his are still like a knife to my own heart.

"Remember, I'll always find you when you really need me."

"Thank you," I whisper.

He gives me his cheekiest grin and dissolves right before my eyes.

"Why are you thanking me?" Zeke asks.

"I wasn't. I was thanking Eli. He found me and stayed with me the whole time I was with Kristoff. I wouldn't have survived without him."

"Eli?" Dan asks, confused. "Eli's dead, baby."

"Yes, but he said he was my Guardian Angel, and that bond transcends death. I needed him, and he found me. He helped me to fight Kristoff in my head. He pushed me to be the old Mattie, to go to the dark place in my mind. Then he brought me Mama because he knew I needed the one person who wouldn't tell me killing Kristoff and Alice was okay, that it wasn't okay if I killed Dan. She's my moral compass." I hold out my hand, and she takes a hesitant step forward. Zeke stiffens beneath me. He hates her. "Papa, be nice."

"Of course, Emma Rose. She's your...mother." He sounds like he's been forced to chew cat poo when he says that, and I laugh.

Disentangling myself from him, I go back to my mama.

God, I miss her so much. I need her. It's a hard thing to love someone so deeply but hate them equally as much. She tried to kill me. To protect me, but it's a hard thing to overcome.

"How long can you stay?"

"A while, baby girl. Eli, he made a deal with someone so I could be here to help you get yourself back to you. The darkness is still there, isn't it?"

"Yes, but it's not the darkness I'm afraid of. It's this place in my head. It's cold and completely white. My emotions are gone when I'm there. I feel them trying to break through, but it's hard. It was easier to let them in before…"

"Before you killed that woman?"

"I don't want to feel this pain, to feel what it means to have hurt her."

"And you went back there?"

I nod.

"You'll be okay, baby girl. I promise. Why don't you let me help you get cleaned up?"

"But Kristoff—"

"We'll deal with Kristoff." Saidie and her motley crew have somehow made their way down here. "Killing him is out of the question since he's gone and bound himself to the girl. We need to find a way to break the human servant bond before we end him."

"There is no way to break that bond." Silas studies his fingernails. "The only way to break it is through death."

"We'll see about that." Saidie smiles, and it reminds me of one of my smiles.

"He's going to be easy to deal with right now," I tell her. "All his bones are crushed."

"That was hella cool." Saidie walks over to us. "Who's this?"

"This is my mama, Claire Hathaway."

"You're dead." Saidie leans in closer and sniffs. "But you're not dead either. It's like you're straddling both sides of the plane. You're here, and you're solid, but at the same time, you have a foot in the afterlife too. How?"

"A Guardian Angel told me my baby girl needed me, and here I am."

"Love can conquer death." I know this to be true. I've pulled Dan from death twice.

"Come on, cupcake, you stink, and you look like something out of a horror move. Let's go get you cleaned up."

With that, Mama pulls me from the mess downstairs and up to my room where she helps me clean up, and after my shower, she lies down on the bed with me.

"Do you have to go, Mama?"

"I don't know how to stay, baby girl."

"Would you want to stay if you could?"

"That's not possible, cupcake."

"But it is."

I know it. The knowledge is there.

"How?"

"I'm Death, but I'm also Creation. I can pull you here, keep you here, but I won't if you don't want to. I can do it before I get Rhea to lock all this away."

"Why don't you try to sleep, cupcake, and we'll talk about it when you wake up?"

"You won't leave while I'm asleep?"

"No. I won't."

"I'm afraid to sleep, Mama. I'm afraid I'll see what I did to Mrs. Banks. I loved her."

"Don't blame yourself for that. Blame Kristoff. He had this planned. He needed someone on the inside, and he bit her before you ever left this house to go to him. He instructed her to hide Dan where no one would see. Eric saw her, and then she had to dispose of him too. Jameson was under Kristoff's thrall as well. He bit them both. Jameson helped her hide them."

"How do you know all this?"

"I saw it. I keep a watch on this house. I was terrified of what Ezekiel would do to you, and I can't shake that feeling. I'll always watch over you."

"Papa will never hurt me. He loves me."

She makes a humming noise but doesn't agree. She spent the last years of her life hiding me from him, afraid he'd kill me. It will take some time for her to get past that, I think.

"I'm sorry I hate you."

"Don't be sorry, baby girl. I deserve your hate. If I hadn't been on drugs, that never would have happened. It's me who's sorry."

"I love you too. I forgave you, and I thought the hate went away until I saw you standing there earlier. All that anger came back, punched right through the wall of ice I had up. I don't want to hate you."

"One day, I hope you can truly forgive me and that hate goes away. But until then, I'm okay with you hating me. Mama loves you, cupcake, and that will never change no matter what is in your heart."

Her words should matter, but I'm caught between the here and now and that cold, emotionless place. Maybe in a few days that place will recede back into my head and I'll process what we said here. Maybe then it'll matter.

There's a knock at the door.

"Come in."

Nathaniel, Mary, Eric, Ethan, and Dan come in. They all look harried.

"I swear to God, if you do that again, I am going to beat you myself." Nathaniel shakes his head. "You scared ten years off me."

"I love you too, Nathaniel." It comes automatically, and I know it's true. I don't feel it like I should, but I know truth in this white noise. And I love my brother.

He goes completely still and stares at me. Mary nudges him, and he shakes his head, like he's trying to clear it.

"It's okay if you can't say it back. I love you enough for both of us."

"I...you really mean it, don't you? You love me, and you don't want anything from me in return."

"That's what love is, Nathaniel. Loving with your whole heart and never judging or leaving, even when it's hard. It's okay to let me love you, to let all of us love you."

Dan slaps him on the back. "Welcome to the family, Nathaniel." Then he crawls into bed beside me, his front to my back. "He's right, though. Don't ever do that again, Squirt. You scared the hell out of all of us."

"Swear jar," I whisper.

Dan chuckles. "There's my girl."

"I'm not the same girl anymore. I went to that cold place, and I killed Mrs. B. I'll never be the same girl again."

"That's okay too, Mattie. We'll love you no matter who you are. You're my girl, and that's all that matters. We'll get you back in therapy, and we'll support you while you heal." Mary sits down on the bed. "Thank you for saving my mom."

"She's a good mom. She took care of me when I needed it. I wasn't letting anyone hurt Mrs. C." I clear my throat, and an old memory of her limping comes to mind. It bothers me. "Mary?"

"Yeah?"

"Do you want me to heal you?"

"Heal me?"

"The scars, your leg…do you want me to make them go away? I can with just a touch."

Tears spring to her eyes. "I do, Mattie, more than anything, but you can't."

"I can."

"No." She shakes her head emphatically. "You told me what Rhea said about healing people. It uses energy from your soul, and I think right now, your soul is tattered and bleeding from everything that's happened to you. I don't want you to be hurt trying to heal me."

I'd forgotten about that. Rhea said healing people was dangerous.

"I healed the Blackburne girl."

"You shouldn't have…" Mary shakes her head. "No more healing until we learn more about it."

"I won't be able to when I ask Rhea to take this away, to lock it back up."

"I've learned to accept who I am with the scars, Mattie. I'm okay."

I don't think she is, but it's her choice. I won't force anything on her.

"Uh, Emm…er…Mattie, can I ask you something?"

"What?" I ask Ethan warily. He's sometimes a little too excited about the supernatural.

"Are you still seeing death dates?"

"Yes."

"You saw them when you looked at the witches?"

"I did."

"You know when they're going to die?"

"That's what the death dates mean."

"So…"

"You don't need to know that information."

"What about—"

"I'm not telling you when anyone is going to die, Ethan. It's not something you should know. Only a reaper should know that."

He looks disappointed, but I don't care. He needs to get his head out of the clouds and take the supernatural world more seriously, more cautiously. He'll be the one we're burying sooner rather than later if he doesn't.

Claire looks around. "You all look ready to drop. Why don't you get some rest, and we'll deal with all of this tomorrow?"

"Yeah, that sounds like a good idea." It's only when Ethan speaks that I notice he's wrapped around Eric like Dan's wrapped around me.

"You two finally figure out what we've known for months?"

Eric blushes. "Yeah, we came to an understanding."

"I'm glad." There's a warmth in my chest, and I think it's happiness, but I'm not sure.

"Thanks."

"Come on. Pile in, and let's get some sleep."

Mama looks surprised. "We're like a pack, Mama. We sleep better when we're all together. We feel safe here. You're safe here."

Once they're all snuggled into my

massive bed, my eyes flutter closed, but I catch movement out of the corner of my eyes. Cass is hanging out by the door.

"Cass?"

He jumps, startled. "Uh…sorry, I didn't mean to eavesdrop."

"It's okay, Cass. You're part of our family too. Everything that was said meant you too."

"You're my sister."

His expression is hesitant, like he can't believe it. Like he doesn't want to believe it. Has to be the demon blood he's having issues with. None of us like having it, but he'll learn to deal with it.

"I am your sister."

"I doan know wha' to say or do…"

"Don't say or do anything tonight. Come and get some rest. There's room." Thank God Zeke saw I needed a bigger bed. This thing is huge. It could probably hold more than ten people.

He shuffles into the room, looking nervous. "How are you feelin'? I know how hard is to come back from dat place."

"Part of me is still there, but everyone

here is helping pull me back. I need all of you. I can't be alone or I'll be that same girl Dan met in the hospital. The girl who had no one and didn't understand she deserved to be loved. I was cold and calculated. I did horrible things. I had to be that girl to survive Kristoff, but I'm trying to come back from her. I'm trying to be a blend of us. I can't cut her out, because she's a part of me. Everyone here helps me temper that girl, helps me temper my darkness. I need them. I need my mama, and I need you, Cass. You're my brother, and I love you. I loved you before I knew you were my brother. You were family, blood or not. You'll always be my family."

"Dude, lay down," Ethan yawns. "We need to sleep. Tomorrow is soon enough to deal with the mess outside the room."

Cass closes the door and crawls into the pile of bodies.

"Emma?"

"Hmm?"

"I love you too."

"I know."

And with that, I close my eyes and fall

into a deep, dreamless sleep.

Saidie

Once Emma goes upstairs, the rest of us are left with the mess.

Specifically, Kristoff.

Who is my mess to deal with, anyway.

"What do we do with him?" Alex asks once the Cranes depart.

"I have no idea. How long will it take him to heal from crushed bones?"

"Wit' a human servant? No' long enough." Aleric squats beside the bloody mess of a vampire. "Hello, bro'der."

"Runt," Kristoff wheezes. "Missed you."

Aleric spits in his face.

"Cold." Cass stands from where he's sitting beside the vampire. "I need to check on Alice, and then I'll come help you with this." He gestures to the vampire before stepping outside.

Sabien comes down the stairs. He blinks when he sees Kristoff, but other than that, he shows no surprise.

"Where is everyone?"

He missed the show. He and Alesha both. They were upstairs with Jason. Cass said his Alpha friend is supposed to come help Jase, but so far, he hasn't shown up. Or he came during the shit show and ran away. Either way, Jason's in a lot of pain, and I am not sure he'll last much longer. The bird thing tore him to shreds.

Strangely, he doesn't even ask what happened, just where everyone is.

"Emma went upstairs with her dead mother, Cass is outside on the phone, and everyone else is checking on the housekeeper, who Emma stabbed to protect her boyfriend."

Again, Sabien just blinks.

What can you really say to that, though?

"Why is this thing not dead?" He doesn't get near the vampire when he asks the question.

"Because he's attached himself to a human servant, a friend of Cass's."

"That's a complication," Sabien replies.

"We're trying to figure out what to do with him."

"I have a room in the vault just for vampires. Alesha and I were planning on capturing one to use for experimentation. Spells to protect against or to harm them are hard to come by without a live one to practice on."

"You cain't be practicin' on Kristoff. You hurt him, you hurt Alice."

"Of course we wouldn't practice on him, Aleric. We wouldn't harm an innocent."

"But you'd harm one of us. No' all vampires are bad. Some of us just want to be left alone."

Sabien's lips purse. "It's not that simple, Aleric."

"But it is."

"Getting him back to West Virginia is

going to be a problem." I insert myself into the conversation before it really goes off the rails. I know Aleric is thinking of Lucien and his other brother. They were always kind to him.

"Dere be a way." Aleric's expression is still quite hostile. "Madame had a coffin she used when she wanted to punish us longer den a few hours. It's spelled so dat we couldn't escape it. She'd keep us in dere for weeks sometimes."

"That would work." Sabien accepts the change of subject. "Do you know where it is?"

"It's in one of de rooms in de basement."

I so do not want to go back to that island, but I won't let Aleric go by himself. It houses too many bad memories.

"I'll go get it," Sabien volunteers. "You two should stay with Jason and the others."

As cold as Sabien can be about certain things, he understands what that island means for Aleric. He's not like Alesha. He accepted Luca and Aleric into the family from day one. I don't know if I would say he loves them, per se, but he cares. Sabien wouldn't knowingly put him into a situation that would harm him physically or mentally.

"I'll come with you." Caleb Malone steps out of the shadows and into the hallway. "It might not be safe to go alone."

"It's perfectly safe," I tell him, my heart speeding up, wondering how much he overheard. Does he know what Aleric is? He's a hunter. What if he tries to hunt him?

"Be that as it may, after everything that's happened the last week, I think it's safer for everyone not to go anywhere alone. We don't know how many eyes Kristoff has out there."

"It's fine, Saidie. I could use the company." Sabien gives me a little nod, and I know he's going to ferret out how much Caleb overheard. He can cast a memory spell on the man if necessary.

Sabien doesn't give him time to go upstairs and tell his father where he's going, saying he can contact James from the car. He's not giving Caleb a chance to rat out Aleric, if that is his intention.

"I'll be glad to get home where we're free to say what we want."

"Aye." Aleric's staring down at Kristoff. "He's healin' faster den I t'ought he wou'."

"What do you mean?"

"Look, *Draga*. His stomach is already stitched back toge'der."

Oh, wow. He is healing fast. "Is it because of Alice?"

Aleric nods. "He's pullin' ever'tin he can from her to heal. At dis rate, he might be healed in an hour or two."

"What can we do? We can't let him heal until he's inside that coffin."

Aleric frowns. "Dey be one t'ing. Lucien cou' do it, but I doan know if I can or no'."

"What?"

"Lucien was a master vampire. It's why he cou' create o'der vampires. He was growing into his abilities. One o' dem was to force a vampire to de age it's supposed to be, and wit'out blood, even wit' a human servant, it takes time to come back from dat."

"You're like Lucien, aren't you?"

"Aye."

"Can you do it?"

"I'm no' sure."

"Alex, can you and Luca make sure no one disturbs us?"

Luca nods. He goes to the top of the stairs, and Alex goes down the hallway to where the Cranes and Nathaniel disappeared. They won't let anyone accidentally walk in on us.

"Will this hurt Alice?" I ask.

"I doan know, but I do know it's de only way to keep him from hurting us while we get him to de vault."

Ringing endorsement.

Aleric takes my hand. "I may need your strength, *Draga*. I am not as old as Lucien or as strong yet. Will you help me?"

See, he asked. He didn't just take what he wanted. That's why I will always freely give him what he needs from me as his human servant. He doesn't take me for granted.

"Always."

"So sweet." Kristoff spits blood out of his mouth.

"You shut the hell up." I kick him and take pleasure in it. He's a vile, evil creature who shouldn't exist, but we have to let him live. I'm not happy about it, but I'm not killing Alice just to get rid of Kristoff.

He laughs, and blood bubbles out of his mouth and runs down the side of his face and chin.

"Doan, *Draga*. He is tryin' to get into your head. Doan let him."

None of us have dead man's blood in our systems. While it's harder for a vampire to get in your head if he hasn't drunk from you, it's still possible. I do need to be careful.

Aleric nods and tugs me to him. I always know when he's pulling strength from me. I feel it in the weakening of my limbs, which is why he's holding on to me. I have a feeling this is going to get to worse.

It takes about ten minutes before I feel the change in the air. The scent of death gets stronger, and Aleric seems to be almost glowing as he calls on his own master vampire abilities.

Kristoff groans, and my eyes snap to him. He seems to be shrinking, shriveling up before my eyes. His face becomes hollow and gaunt, his eyes shrinking in their sockets. His skin becomes paper thin and full of wrinkles. He looks like some ancient mummy when Aleric is finished.

I feel like an ancient mummy, I realize as my legs give out and I slide down Aleric's body, landing in a heap at his feet. If I feel like this, what must Alice feel like?

"Come, *Draga*." Aleric reaches down and pulls me into his arms. "You need sugar."

"But Kristoff…"

"We'll watch him," Alex says. "Aleric's right. You don't look so good, Saidie. You need to do what he tells you to."

Aleric carries me into the kitchen where the housekeeper is laid out on the kitchen table. There are bloody towels everywhere, but it doesn't look like she made it.

Aleric ignores everyone and sets me on the kitchen counter. He goes into the fridge and pulls out a container of orange juice. He doesn't even get a glass, just twists off the cap and hands it to me.

Everyone's staring, but I dutifully swallow the sweet juice. It's not my favorite, but according to Aleric, it will pull my blood sugar up faster than anything else. Maybe that's why they give you orange juice after you donate blood.

"Is she all right?" Zeke asks, coming over to us. Aleric growls, and the man is smart enough to stand back.

"I'm fine. I just had to stop Kristoff from healing himself before we could contain him. It took a lot out of me."

"You should rest." Concern is coming off the man in waves. For someone who is supposed to be a criminal mastermind and apathetic when it comes to others in his quest for power, he sure doesn't seem like that in person.

"I will, once we have Kristoff secured in the spelled coffin. Sabien and Caleb went to get it from the island."

Zeke nods. "Has the shifter arrived yet?"

"Not that I know of, but hopefully soon." My eyes shift to the woman on the table. "I'm sorry about your housekeeper."

Zeke's eyes close briefly. "She was family."

Which makes her death at the hands of his daughter all the more painful. I don't know what I'd do or feel in his situation.

"I'm very sorry."

"Thank you, Saidie." He turns to Aleric. "Why don't you take her into my office so she can rest? It's right off the hallway where Kristoff is."

"T'ank you." Aleric hands me the container of juice and picks me up again before heading to the office.

The couch in here is probably the most comfortable couch I've ever sat on. I could fall asleep for hours if I let myself.

"We need a couch like this."

"Aye, *Draga*, we do. Maybe de Cranes will tell us where to ge' one."

"Maybe."

"Are you okay, *bon fille*? I took a lot from you. I didn't wan' to, but it was necessary to put him down."

"I'm just really tired, Aleric, but I'll be fine. I have this whole carton of OJ." I shake the now capped carton at him, and he laughs, even though it's not funny.

"I love you, Saidie."

Aleric doesn't say that often, so when he does, it means that much more to me.

"I love you too, Aleric."

"Close your eyes, *bon fille*. Sleep."

"Kristoff—"

"Is no' going anywhere, and his powers are reduced to mush right now. It's safe to sleep."

Knowing he's right, and because I can barely keep my eyes open, I fall asleep within moments of closing them.

***

The screaming wakes me up.

"What is it?" I ask, jerking up from where I'm lying atop Aleric. "What's wrong?"

"I doan know," he says and helps me to stand. I'm still a little shaky, but I don't let it stop me from rushing out of the room.

Kristoff is no longer in the hallway.

It's more of a side note as another agonized scream rips through the house. Aleric and I hit the top of the stairs together. The hallway is crowded with people, the Richards and the Malone clans, mostly.

"What's wrong?"

"It's the shifter," James Malone says. "They're forcing him to shift and heal."

"His name is Jason."

James just stares me down. He's not happy his daughter is the fated mate of a shifter. Tough. Jason is my friend, my family. He matters more than this man.

I run to his room and throw open the door. Alex and Luca are standing back, Ava Malone held tightly to Alex. Ava looks sickened and scared. She's probably never seen a shifter shift before. It can be disturbing.

A man is standing by the bed, his hand on Jason. The power coming off him is incredible. But then, so is he. He's tall, a scruffy beard covering the lower half of his face, and his eyes are glowing amber with his wolf. Tattoos cover every inch of his arms I can see. He's one of those gorgeous bad boys you read about in romance novels. Only I have a feeling this one is truly a bad, bad man.

"It's done." He steps back, and the amber leaves his eyes, allowing me to see the dark green orbs.

Gorgeous man candy.

"T'ank you, Landon. I know you didn't want to come here, but I appreciate it."

"She was his mate, and he protected her. It's our most basic law to protect our mates. He deserved my help for dat."

Cass shakes his hand and leads the man out of the room.

It's only then Alex lets Ava loose. She runs to the bed, but Jason is finally unconscious. I'm sort of glad I wasn't here for the whole thing. I'm also surprised James allowed Ava to be in here.

"There was no keeping her out," Alex whispers, reading my expression. "If it were Luca, I'd kill someone who tried to keep me away from him while he's in this much pain."

I guess that whole mate bond thing is stronger than I thought when it comes to a human.

"He'll sleep for several days," Alesha tells Ava. "Do you want to wait here with him for a bit?"

She nods, her brown eyes full of tears.

"Ava, have you heard of Appalachia University?" Alex goes to sit down beside the girl on the bed.

"No."

"It's a school in West Virginia. Supernatural creatures and those who know about them go there. It's also a top five school. Jason and I live in the town the school is in."

Ava blinks several times before what Alex is trying to tell her sinks in. "Does he go to school there?"

"Yes, he graduates this May with his bachelor's degree in psychology, but I think he's thinking of getting his master's. The school offers that as well."

"So, I could see him if I attended that

school?"

Alex smiles and strokes the girl's blonde hair. "Yes."

Ava nods and goes back to holding Jason's hand. I think Alex just solved all our problems. Once the girl graduates, her father can't control what she does, at least to a certain degree.

Attending Wolfpack University, as it's lovingly called by the students, is going to be a fight, though. James Malone will know the school's reputation, and allowing his baby girl to attend might not go over so well. She has a bit to convince him, and I'm guessing by the fierce look on her face, she's going to win.

Alex stands and motions me and Aleric to follow her. She ignores the people in the hall as we make our way to her and Luca's room.

"I hate bigots like that," she says as soon as the door closes. "They're racist."

"Racist?"

"They don't think we're good enough because we're shifters."

I'm not sure I'd go that far. It was a shock finding out your baby girl is mated to a shifter when you hunt monsters for a living. It might take them some time to get used to the idea.

"They'll come around."

"How do you know that?"

"Because your brother is a loveable goofball. No one resists his charms for long."

She doesn't look convinced.

"Are you okay?" she asks after a moment. "You looked like death warmed over earlier. At least there's some color back in your cheeks."

"I'm good." I don't mention I'm still dizzy and tired. I can go back to sleep later.

"Good, because I want to tell you something."

"What's wrong now?"

"Nothing's wrong."

"You scared me, Alex. Kristoff was missing from downstairs and I thought he might have escaped…"

"No, nothing like that. Uncle Sabien and Caleb loaded him up and are taking him to West Virginia now. Where they found a hearse, I have no idea."

"Then what is it?"

"I think I'm better."

What does she mean, she's better?

"When I touched Emma earlier, I felt something warm, like a hot bath washing over me, and ever since then, I haven't heard my grandfather's voice in my head. I haven't seen images of the other reality trying to crowd out this one. It's just gone."

It's my turn to blink.

"She said she healed me, and I think she did. And it's just not that. I can feel something else, like all the power in my body that's been running rampant seems to have calmed down. I don't know, but I think she did that too. I think she fixed me."

"That's…" I don't even know what to say.

"I can't…" Alex breaks off, and tears start to trickle down her face. "I don't…"

I hug her. It's the only thing I know to do. She hugs me back just as tightly. The spell her grandfather cast on her really did a number on her, and having those effects just gone? I can't even imagine what that must feel like.

"At least one good thing came out of this hellish nightmare, then. I'm glad we came, if for no other reason than you're not having to struggle with what's real."

"Me too."

"Hush, *munya*." Luca extracts her from my hold. "Is okay. Everything is okay."

She only cries harder.

I'm at a loss, but Aleric wisely just takes my hand and leaves the room, shutting Luca and Alex in. Luca will take care of her.

"Let's go to our room."

There's a fierce light in his eyes, and it's one I recognize. He needs me as much as I need him. After the day we've had, it's about the only thing that will help us both come down from the stress we've been under since Emma showed up with Kristoff in tow.

"Promise we'll actually sleep at some point?"

He only smiles and leads me to our room at the other end of the hall.

Sleep may or may not come for several hours, but I'm fine with that.

Emma/Mattie

Morning brings a whole bag of problems, but when I wake up, it's just me and Dan. Everyone else has vacated.

"Where's Mama?" I look around desperately when I realize she's not here. She promised not to leave.

"It's okay, baby. She went downstairs to help Heather cook for everyone. She didn't leave you."

My whole body sags with relief. She didn't leave me.

Dan rolls so he's got me caged in. "You scared me, Squirt. I know why you did what you did, but next time, tell me, and we'll figure it out. I can't lose you, Mattie. Please don't ever do that to me again. Please."

Taking his face in my hands, I pull him down for a kiss. I put everything in that kiss that I can't put into words. I show him my fear, my rage, my anger, my grief. I show him how he saved me time and time again. I show him the courage he gave me, and I show him how much I love him.

"I love you, Mattie Louise Hathaway," he whispers raggedly when he comes up for air. "I love you more than my own life."

He does. I feel it in a way I've never felt anything. As I slept last night, surrounded by the people who love me, more and more of that cold place slipped away. It's not gone, but it let me start to feel things.

And I know one truth with perfect clarity.

We are our choices. Mama was right about that. I chose time and time again to keep people at arm's length, to keep them away so they can't hurt me. Even Dan.

To a degree.

He asked me a question, and I said yes, but with stipulations. I hate change. Marrying him would be a big change and one I was scared of. He knew it when I didn't. He's always content to let me lead, to let me come to terms with the changes I'm afraid of.

But as a reaper who sees everyone's death dates, I also know our time here is shorter than we think, and we need to embrace it, to live our lives like every moment is our last.

I can't be afraid of change. I have to give in to it and let myself be happy. I have to try, anyway.

And it starts with one big change.

"Marry me, Dan."

He tilts his head. "I already asked you that, baby."

"No, I know. What I mean is marry me now, sooner than two or three years from now. Seeing you really dead, lying there in a pool of your own blood...I don't know. It broke me. And then Eric...I ripped his head off his body...I can't lose you like that again, Dan. I can't."

"Shhh…" He rolls again, bringing us face to face. "We're both fine, baby. There's no need to rush. You're reacting to what happened. I want you to marry me when you're ready, not because you're afraid."

"That's the point. I saw so many things when those doors opened in my mind. I saw futures, so many different paths, but they all led back to you. It doesn't matter if I marry you today or tomorrow or three years from now. I want to belong to you in every single way. I want to be Mattie Richards."

"Mattie Crane Richards." He rubs his nose alongside mine. "Your father has already insisted upon that before he'd give me his blessing."

I laugh softly. "Leave it to Zeke to insist upon his name stamped all over me."

"He lost you for fifteen years, Mattie. I understand what that feels like. You've gone missing on me twice, and both times I nearly lost my mind."

"I know what it feels like too. I held you while you were bleeding out. I reached inside to a part of me that scares me to keep you with me. When I saw you die…when Ralph killed you…"

"He didn't, baby. I'm fine."

"I'm not." I close my eyes and see the knife flying toward Mrs. Banks. "I killed Mrs. B. I'm not fine." The tears hitch in my voice, and he presses into me, covering me with his entire body. "I guess my attempt at no rap sheet in New Orleans just went out the window."

"No, sweetheart, you're not being arrested."

"But I killed Mrs. Banks, Dan. Of course they're going to arrest me."

"No, baby, they're not. James and your father are taking care of it."

"I…Dan…you can't…you're a cop…"

He kisses my forehead. "It was self-defense of another person. You were protecting me. Zeke and James have already spoken to the district attorney, and he's agreed no charges will be pressed."

"He had time to do all that?"

"Baby, it's mid-afternoon. You've slept all night and all day."

"I…I don't know what to say. How do I go down there and face everyone?"

"The same way you always do. With that fierceness that you always approach everything with. It's why I love you. You never back down. Ever."

"Kristoff messed with my head. He got me so twisted…what I did to Ralph…"

"Who is Ralph, baby?"

"His ghoul. He was dead, but he looked alive. He functioned like any living person. I saw him slit your throat, and I couldn't stop it. And then I attacked him. I ripped his head off, only it was Eric."

"It wasn't real, baby. It was just a trick."

"I know. But I slaughtered Ralph. I ripped him apart with my bare hands, and I enjoyed it, Dan. I'm afraid of myself. Part of me is still there, and it's tempering what I'm feeling now. If I felt everything, I don't think I could function. I don't want to be in that cold place, though, but I don't know how to leave it completely behind. What if I can't ever leave it behind?"

"I'll always be here to pull you back, baby. I'll learn a summoning spell to bring your mother back to us so she can pull you out if I can't."

"You'd really do that?"

"Yes. I don't know how I feel about her being here. She tried to kill you. Part of me hates her for that, and it's all I can do not to pull my sword and let it judge her. And then there's Zeke. He's almost bitten his tongue off twice. He doesn't want her here. She took you from him, Mattie. He wants her here about as much as you want to eat broccoli. I have to agree with him. I don't want her here."

I know part of that is because of his mother, who shot him to hurt me. He can't forgive her or get past it. Maybe one day he will, but I honestly don't care if he never does, so I understand his hatred too. I hate his mother.

"I hate her too, but I love her. I forgave her a long time ago. She killed to protect me. I did the same thing last night. I killed to protect you. I'm afraid when you realize what that means, you'll leave. You'll run far and away."

"Is that why you want to get married now? You're afraid I'll leave you?"

"I—"

"Don't you get it, Squirt? I'm never leaving, no matter what you do. You can't get rid of me. I've stuck by you through everything. You're the other half of my soul. I could no more cut you out of my life than I can strip out my soul. You're mine, and no one, not even you, is taking you away from me."

"Do you mean that?"

"I do. God, Mattie, I went a little crazy when you left, and then when I felt the pain you were going through…"

"Wait, you felt that? How? I couldn't feel you at all. The choke collar he had around my neck cut me off from everything. I couldn't even see the ghosts. I could feel them, though. The collar cut me off from my abilities, but it couldn't shut off what was inside. I'm so sorry you had to feel all that."

"One of the witches put me in a dreamless sleep after a few hours. I was asleep for almost a week."

"I'm glad they did that. You didn't

need to feel that pain."

"We'll call your therapist. Think that'll help?"

"Yeah. I need to talk to someone. Someone who isn't you or the rest of my family. You guys don't need to understand the monster inside me."

"I love the monster too. It's part of you, Squirt. The sooner you accept that, the sooner you'll start to heal."

Maybe he's right. I don't know.

"Where were you? We looked everywhere."

"Fulsome Sanitarium in Missouri. It was an abandoned insane asylum. The ghosts there were dangerous. Kristoff had coated one of the basement rooms in iron so they couldn't get in. It was the only safe room in the building. But I wasn't safe. Every time I slept, Kristoff took my memories and turned them into nightmares. He fed from me every day, and I got weaker and weaker until I could barely keep my eyes open. I sank into that horrible nightmare world, and it broke me a little more every day."

"How did you get out?"

"When I saw you guys die, it flipped a switch. A switch I've only ever flipped once before. I went to the cold place in my head I told you about, the place where there is no pain, no grief, no anything. I knew what to do. I guess maybe I knew all along, but I kept waiting for someone to save me."

"We tried, baby."

I put a finger to his lips. "Eli was there. He kept telling me to survive I had to be the old Mattie. I didn't want to be her, but when you and Eric died, I knew I was on my own, and I did what he told me to do. I went back to that place. I called Peaches, and she bit the collar off me."

"Silas said Peaches couldn't…"

"No one could have sent her after me, but when I call her, she comes."

"You should have done that earlier."

"He showed me a live feed of Ava. He had eyes on her. I couldn't do anything to get her hurt."

"He played on your fears."

"He did. So, I stayed and played his games, which mostly happened when I was sleeping. When he fed from me, he broke bones. He cut me with a knife that looked like the knife the day Mama…" I break off, unable to voice it. "Please don't ask me anything else today, Dan. I'll tell you all of it when I can, but no more today."

"It's okay. You can tell me when you're ready. And we can get married when you're ready, Squirt. There's no rush. I'm here, I'm alive, and I'm not going anywhere."

"How can I explain this so you'll understand?" I run my fingers through his messy hair and pull him down so I can feel his cheek against mine. The stubble from where he hasn't shaved scratches my face, and I rub my cheek against it. I love it when he has stubble.

"I understand, Squirt. You're scared, and you've been through a terrible ordeal. You're trying to find ways to…"

"Shhh," I shush him. "I'm not trying to overcompensate, if that's what you were going to say. I've thought long and hard on this, Dan. While I was down there in that basement, when I saw you die…it all culminated into one truth. I love you more than I love anyone, more than I love myself, and I want everyone to know that. I want to marry you, Dan. Not two years from now, but two weeks from now, tops. I want to be your wife more than anything. Unless you don't want to marry me?" The thought sends chills down my spine.

"No, Mattie. I wouldn't have asked if I didn't want you to be my wife. I love you the same way, more than I do myself, which is why I think you're reacting. I think you need to think about this. Think long and hard."

"I'm done thinking, Dan. I want to marry you. I love you. That's not going to change, so why does it matter if we get married sooner rather than later?"

"Why does it matter if we wait?"

"Because tomorrow is not promised, Dan. I see it every single time I look at someone who's scheduled to die today. I see it when my bones shudder with the knowledge of their death. I want to live today like it's our last, like we know tomorrow isn't promised. I want us to live, Dan, not be afraid. Let's live for today. Marry me."

"You're serious."

"I am, and I want Mama there. She can only be here for a short time. I want my mama at my wedding, Dan."

"When do you want to get married, Squirt?"

"Like I said, no more than two weeks from now. You can request vacation time later for a honeymoon. I just want to be your wife."

"Okay, baby, if this is what you really want, we'll get married in two weeks, but Lila is gonna have a heart attack."

"She might."

"Ready to go tell her?"

"Do I have to? Can't you do it?"

"Uhhhh, no. She's your grandmother. You're not escaping."

"Fine." I push him, and he rolls off me so I can throw the covers back and sit up. It only takes me ten minutes in the bathroom, and then we go downstairs. Everyone is in the dining room waiting. It's like a round table full of King Arthur's knights.

Mama sees me and gets up, pulling me

into a hug. "Feel better, cupcake?"

I missed that old nickname. I loved cupcakes. She bought a package of them once, and I ate the whole thing. My face was covered in chocolate and frosting. She started calling me cupcake right after that.

"I'm better."

Zeke looks fit to be tied, but he'd better get used to it. Mama is part of my life. She loves me as much as he does.

"Come sit. I'll get you some food."

Dan leads me to a chair, and I take my seat, very aware of all the stares leveled at me. They probably have a thousand and one questions. I only have one.

"Is Jameson okay?"

"Yes. He was injured and is in the hospital. He gets to come home tomorrow. They just want to keep him another night for observation. We found him in the maze this morning." Zeke fidgets with the pen in his hand.

"And Kristoff?"

"He's already in West Virginia," Saidie says. "Sabien and Caleb Malone took him late last night."

"That's good. You're sure he won't be able to get out?"

"No, I swear. Sabien's been planning for this since Madame died. I knew eventually I would have to come down here and deal with him, but I never expected him to find a human servant."

"No one did."

"At least the island is cleared of all monsters. There was a woman named Rhea who came and took care of it…" She trails off when Rhea appears to the left of me.

"Hello, Saidie." She gives her one of those brilliant smiles that stuns people before turning to me. "Rose. You look better."

"I am better, thank you."

"You found your reaper friend?"

"I did. He's safe now. It's going to take a lot for him to heal."

She nods and looks around, but her expression stutters when she sees Mama walking back into the room carrying a plate with a double bacon cheeseburger and fries. My mouth waters at the sight.

Right on cue, my stomach grumbles

loudly. I blush, but hey. I'm hungry. I haven't eaten in days.

"Here you go, baby girl. Mary told me this is your favorite, so I made them for lunch, but you slept straight through."

"That's okay, Mama. Old burgers are just as good as fresh ones." I take a huge bite, and the little moan that slips out is even more embarrassing. God, I missed real food.

"Told you she does that," Benny whispers to Brandon, Cameron's son. Cam and his father are not here. Neither is Cam's wife, Amy.

"Where's your brother and Amy?"

"Cam is with Amy. He took her to her job interview this morning."

Job interview?

"At the hospital. She applied this morning when she saw they were looking for nurses, and they asked her to come in this afternoon for an interview. They've lost over a dozen nurses in the last month."

"Why?"

"Don't know."

"And your dad?"

"He had court."

I pop a fry in my mouth and groan as the sweet, ketchupy taste hits my tongue.

"The bottomless pit speaks." Benny giggles, and his mother shushes him.

"We have some news we want to share," Dan says nervously. His gaze cuts to Lila and Josiah, who are on either side of Zeke at the head of the table. "Good news Mattie wants to tell you about."

I let out a burp when he elbows me to speak. "Coward," I mouth at him. He nods like he's quite serious, and maybe he is. I don't know.

"We're getting married."

My family looks confused.

Josiah is the first one to speak. "We know that, honey."

"No, I mean we're getting married within two weeks."

Utter and complete silence.

This isn't good.

Benny is the first one to react. He jumps up and comes over to hug me. "You're gonna be my sister for real now."

I smile at the kid. "Yeah, you don't

mind me marrying your brother?"

"Nah." He gives me a sloppy kiss on the cheek and rambles back to his seat, filching a fry off my plate in the process.

"*Ma petite*, I'm not sure now is the right time to be getting married." Zeke's hand clenches. "After what you've been through…it's normal to do crazy things. Maybe you should hold off for a while."

"Two weeks gives me no time to plan a wedding!" Lila nearly screeches. "There's the dress, the venue, the food, the flowers…"

"Are you saying you can't pull it off, *Grandmère*?"

"I never said that. I'm Lila Crane. I will pull it off."

"Why the rush?" Heather Malone asks.

"Because I realized that life is short, and I know that Dan is the only man I will ever love enough to marry. I'd rather live my life now than wait and worry and live in fear. I want to be his wife, and there's no reason to wait. I want my mama at the wedding. I want all of you at the wedding. That includes you, Saidie, and everyone from West Virginia."

I turn to Rhea, who looks uncomfortable. "I want you there too, Rhea. You deserve to see your daughter married as much as Mama does."

She swallows and runs a hand through my hair. "You've never called yourself my daughter before."

"Let's just say what I went through put a lot of things into perspective for me." I turn back to the room. "It's going to be a long time before I'm back to normal, but I want things around me to be normal. That means all of you doing what you normally do, and I'm hoping, Alesha, you might be able to suggest a trustworthy witch we could employee at The Hathaway Foundation."

"That is the foundation for the hunters?"

"It is. We spent a small fortune on spells. It would be easier to have a witch on staff who gets paid a monthly salary instead of letting people rip us off. And I'm fairly sure the last one did."

"I could do it until I can locate someone else. I need to go through our family home here in New Orleans, anyway."

"Really?" I know she is highly respected in the witch community, at least according to Zeke.

"Sure. It would only be temporary, though. My children come first. We're just getting to know each other again. I won't leave them for longer than necessary."

"Of course. I appreciate it. Once we find a permanent location with enough room to build out like we want to, we'll get set up. Our corporate offices are in town, but I want the foundation to be away from everything. I want it to be a second home for the hunters, a place we can build a dorm for the kids and a school. Hunters need a safe place to leave their kids."

"The same hunters who didn't lift a finger to help you?" Nathaniel seethes. "Those hunters?"

"Yes, Nathaniel. They'll come around."

I know it. I've seen it.

Everywhere I look, everyone I look at, I see their futures. I see the many paths they can take and where they'll end up. Well, except for the Blackburnes and the people with them. Their fates are not written. It's odd, but I decide not to question it. There's enough to worry about without that.

The hunters are my main concern. It's going to be a long road, but the they are going to come around. And Cass has a lot to do with that. He just doesn't know it. I can't tell him either. It might affect the outcome. It's hard knowing things and not being able to say anything.

"Why don't I give you the island?" Saidie asks. "It's over a hundred acres out in the swamp. There's plenty of land and a house. Madame's things transferred to me, and I don't want them. Rhea got rid of all the monsters. It would be perfect."

It *would* be perfect.

"How much do you want for it?"

"Call it a wedding present. I never wanted it to begin with."

"Thank you."

"You're welcome."

"Emma Rose, I need to speak with

you." Zeke stands and waits for me.

I eye my food. Best to get this over with. I know he's freaking out.

I walk with him outside to the gardens. He pulls me into a hug before I can even speak. It's so tight it cuts off my air.

"You are never to do that again. Do you understand me?"

"Yes, Papa. I promise never to do that again. Where's Nancy?"

"She went home. When the bird thing attacked Jason and Ava yesterday, I think it really got to her. She's going to have to decide if she can handle our world."

There's a deep pain in his voice and in his eyes. "Don't worry, Papa. Nancy is stronger than you think. She'll come around."

"She is one of the few women who won't let me by with anything. She calls me out on everything."

"She loves you, Papa. Give her time. It's not easy having your entire world ripped apart. It took Dan three days to come talk to me after I told him I could see ghosts."

"I hope you're right."

"She will come around, Papa."

He lets out a sigh and loosens his hold on me. "Are you sure about this? It seems sudden and rash. You could wait a few months…"

"I'm sure, Papa. I want to be Dan's wife. I know we're young, but even you have to admit, Dan and I are it for each other. Why wait? Why not just get married and enjoy it while we're young? We can be Grumpy Gusses forty years from now. I want this, Papa."

"Okay, *ma petite*. I will open my checkbook and let Lila plan the grandest wedding this town has ever seen."

"I would say I want a small wedding, but I think I've sprung enough surprises on Lila for one day."

Zeke laughs. "Yes, she was already going into general mode when we left."

"I want Mama there. Is that a problem for you?"

"I will never forgive that woman for taking you from me, but I will handle it. You love her. She took care of you as best she could. Will she be able to stay that long, though?"

"Every door in my head unlocked when Alex Reed touched me. All of them. I can keep her here for as long as she wants to stay."

"Is it a good idea for you to do that? The last time a good portion of your powers surfaced, it almost killed you."

"I'll have Rhea lock them back up after the wedding and heal whatever damage is done."

"You've got this all figured out, don't you?"

"All except for the part where I killed Mrs. B. I can't get past it, Papa. Dan wants me to call my therapist, and I agreed. It's eating me up inside. I can't even think about it because I...it hurts, Papa. I loved her."

"I know, my beautiful, beautiful girl. She knows you didn't mean to do it. She whispered that to me. To tell you she forgives you."

"She did?"

"She did. She'd want you to move past it."

"I can't just put it behind me, no matter how brave I'm trying to look in front of everyone. I'm broken, Papa. I don't know if that piece of me will ever heal, the piece that took the life of someone I loved."

"It doesn't heal. I've taken the life of someone I valued, a friend who was loyal. A curse caused him to try to kill everyone, and I had to put him down. It nearly killed me, but I worked through it just as you will. I promise you'll get through this. I'm right here. We're all here for you, sweetheart."

"Thank you, Papa."

"What say we go inside and rile up Lila with a deadline of fourteen days to put on the wedding of the century?"

"Sounds like a plan."

I hide my face in his shirt until I can rearrange my expression back into the impish one I'd used before. The mask I hide my pain behind. I will deal with it later.

Right now, we have a wedding to plan.

ABOUT THE AUTHOR

So who am I? Well, I'm the crazy girl with an imagination that never shuts up. I LOVE scary movies. My friends laugh at me when I scare myself watching them and tell me to stop watching them, but who doesn't love to get scared? I grew up in a small town nestled in the southern mountains of West Virginia where I spent days roaming around in the woods, climbing trees, and causing general mayhem. Nights I would stay up reading Nancy Drew by flashlight under the covers until my parents yelled at me to go to sleep.

Growing up in a small town, I learned a lot of values and morals, I also learned parents have spies everywhere and there's always someone to tell your mama you were seen kissing a particular boy on a particular day just a little too long. So when you get grounded, what is there left to do? Read! My Aunt Jo gave me my first real romance novel. It was a romance titled "Lord Margrave's

Deception." I remember it fondly. But I also learned I had a deep and abiding love of mysteries and anything paranormal. As I grew up, I started to write just that and would entertain my friends with stories featuring them as main characters.

Now, I live Huntersville, NC where I entertain my niece and nephew and watch the cats get teased by the birds and laugh myself silly when they swoop down and then dive back up just out of reach. The cats start yelling something fierce…lol.

I love books, I love writing books, and I love entertaining people with my silly stories.

Facebook:
https://www.facebook.com/authorAprylBaker

Twitter:
https://twitter.com/AprylBaker

Website:
http://www.aprylbaker.com/

Bookbub:
https://www.bookbub.com/authors/apryl-baker

Wattpad:
http://www.wattpad.com/user/AprylBaker7

Newsletter:
https://www.aprylbaker.com/contact

Facebook Fan Page:
https://www.facebook.com/groups/AprylsAngel
s

Instagram:
https://www.instagram.com/apryl.baker

Blog:
https://www.mycrazycornerblog.com/

Amazon:
https://goo.gl/b1br13

Join our Reader Group on Facebook and don't miss out on meeting our authors and entering epic giveaways!

Limitless Reading

Where reading a book is your first step to becoming *limitless...*

LIMITLESS PUBLISHING *Reader Group*

Join today! *"Where reading a book is your first step to becoming limitless..."*

https://www.facebook.com/groups/LimitlessReading/